LOVE'S MASQUERADE

LOVE'S MASQUERADE

Cynthia Richey

Walker and Company
New York, New York

First published in the United States of America in 1990 by
Walker Publishing Company, Inc.
Published simultaneously in Canada by Thomas Allen & Son
Canada, Limited, Markham, Ontario

Library of Congress Cataloging-in-Publication Data

Richey, Cynthia
Love's Masquerade/Cynthia Richey

ISBN 0-8027-1117-0
I. Title.
PS3568.I334L68   1990
813'.54—dc20   89-77857
CIP

Printed in the United States of America
2 4 6 8 10 9 7 5 3 1

= 1 =

GREY EYES SPARKLING in anticipation, Miss Sarah Fairchild broke the wafer on Aunt Anne's letter. Surely it contained the invitation which must end her exile. Breakfast, already laid before her on the damask covered table, could wait. Sarah unfolded the pink vellum and began to read:

> "Dearest Sarah,"
> This summer, instead of going to Brighton, we follow the *beau monde* to London. Darling Sarah, just imagine! The reigning monarchs of the civilised world congregated in London! I should be *desolée* to miss such a crush as that will be!"

London! It was the perfect answer to Sarah's prayers. In London she could find a patron for her school. Hopefully, she read on:

> "I am not so insensitive to your own grieving heart, my dear niece, to subject you to the disturbing sight of military reviews and the vexacious din of concerts and balls so soon after your father's tragic death.
> "What would be a pleasure to some, would only grieve you. I trow you never allow others to depress you with their sorrows, but I am too easily persuaded to others' feelings. I cannot expect our circle to cheer you.

"When you have recovered, we must discuss certain matters which do not make sympathetic reading. I cannot, at any rate, write of your difficulties with equanimity. Christmastime will be soon enough to face such unpleasantness."

Perhaps her aunt thought Christmas soon enough to face the unpleasantness to which Sarah awoke every day. As she finished reading the letter, Sarah realised that she had finally come to the end of her rope.

To be sure, she had no great personal ambitions, aside from instituting a school for young ladies at Fair Meadow. When her father had been killed at Vitoria last June, she had soon realised she must find a source of income, but had been compelled to postpone any plans until her period of mourning was concluded.

Aunt Anne's letter dashed even that hope. Exiled from society as she was in Northamptonshire, Sarah could not apply to those among the *ton* who were considered to have philanthropic interests. She sighed. There was nothing left to do. She must sell Fair Meadow.

Though she had been hungry when she sat at table, the letter and its consequences—her disappointment and feelings of impending panic—had robbed her of any appetite. She placed the letter beside her plate. The woman who had served as her abigail for more than ten years gazed with ill-disguised interest at the half-open letter, then at Sarah with excitement. "Your year of isolation is over, Miss; how soon shall we be travelling to Brighton?"

Sarah's moistened lips had gone dry. "Aunt Anne is for London this summer, Trent; and we shall not go," Sarah replied, desperately attempting to keep her countenance from revealing too much disappointment. "Aunt has kindly suggested the frivolity might be too vexing."

Clucking her tongue reprovingly, Trent poured coffee into a delicate cup and placed it before her employer. Sarah regarded her apprehensively. The maid, who was more like

2

a companion to her, was sometimes too free with her tongue. "Pah. Lady Anne never wastes herself on vexations that don't concern her. More likely her ladyship won't put herself out for you."

Sarah frowned disapproval at her abigail's outspoken criticism. That she was right did not excuse the uncharitable remark. "How unkind in you. Aunt is rather concerned that I will not like the noisiness of Town after a year of solitude. So I shall stay home." Sarah stirred sugar into her coffee. The spoon tinkled merrily against the porcelain. She attempted to make her voice sound light. "It is of little consequence. There is always the Little Season."

Sarah presented a brave front, but she knew full well there would be no other Season in London. Thanks to her aunt's insensitivity, she must, sooner or later, be compelled either to live on that relative's doubtful charity or to find a position as governess to the spoiled offspring of some well-off family. Neither prospect raised her spirits. She felt sad, as though she had disappointed her father's hopes by letting Fair Meadow fall into disrepair after his untimely death. (Although where the money was to be found to bring the estate to its former state of efficiency and comfort, she did not know.) She sighed, forgetting for a moment her resolve to keep up appearances before her servants who would not abandon her in these dark days. She was startled out of her brown study by Trent.

"Not to go?" exclaimed the maid, standing with her hands on her hips. It was her "over my dead body" stance. Sarah knew from experience that her abigail did not mean to take this disappointment lying down. She was compelled to conceal an indulgent smile behind a shapely hand when Trent enquired, "If you will pardon me, Miss, how does Lady Anne deny you? Doesn't she understand your position?"

The thought of her position very nearly reduced Sarah to tears. In a watery voice, she said, "I am rather requested to understand hers." Clenching her slender hand into a fist, she lay it in her lap and vowed she would not give into futile expressions of despair. Such whimperings were unbefitting the daughter of Sir Henry Fairchild. Taking a sip of coffee, she finally succeeded in controlling the trembling of her lower lip. "I suppose she does not feel quite up to sponsoring me in addition to my cousins."

"That I can believe," Trent remarked. She was smoothing a cloth over the mahogany tea safe as though it was her sole responsibility to keep her employer's possessions from going to rack and ruin. "Those two country misses will have her ladyship in a taking over their passion for officers." Applying the cloth to the window frame, she continued in a conversational tone, "T'wouldn't surprise me if one of them hightailed it to Gretna Green."

"Phoebe and Chloe are vivacious; not reckless." Sarah thought indulgently of her cousins as girls, although they were younger than she by a mere two and three years. Why neither of them had yet married puzzled her, for they never lacked for dancing partners and were always surrounded by gentlemen eager to turn their heads with a compliment.

Trent seemed to have ceased to wonder at the Severn girls' lack of success in the Marriage Mart, for she said, "Your cousins are desperate to marry, and are not above using tricks to get their hearts' desire. A gentleman knows when a girl thinks of him as a prize to be bagged."

Sarah began to laugh heartily. "Do stop. I shan't be able to visit my cousins without thinking of them shooting pigeons."

Tucking her dustcloth in the pocket of her apron, Trent said with a twinkle in her blue eyes, "They prefer bores."

The pair were caught up by merry laughter, which pealed forth in waves whenever either of them repeated the pun. Finally, her sides aching, Sarah felt the humour dissolve as quickly as it had erupted. In its place was the distressing image of her future. She was forced to admit her unhappy prospects. "That may well be, but as I have no skill in luring unwary game into my net, we shall have to make do until Mr. Quoinby finds a buyer for Fair Meadow."

She saw Trent's jaw tense and knew once more that her companionable abigail was about to fire another verbal salvo. "Arthur Quoinby has brought this house nothing but bad news ever since Sir Henry, God rest him, was killed. I know I'm speakin' out of place, Miss, but I'm out of patience with him and all who plague you."

"Calm yourself, Trent," Sarah said soothingly, but she might have saved her breath.

"I'm of a mind to go to London myself, and tell your aunt to her face what I think of this state of affairs."

Sarah raised a forbidding, but weary hand. "I wish you will not. Aunt does not mean it unkindly."

Trent sniffed and said, "Maybe not, but I'm takin' it unkindly. Since y'r mother died, God rest her, Lady Anne has always wanted you beholden to her. Don't know why, seein's how she never showed the least interest in you before then." She was jabbing her long forefinger in the air for emphasis. "She knows as well as I what that letter means."

Sarah laid her spoon on the saucer and raised her chin in a manner which suggested she had heard too much. "How can you say that? Aunt stands to lose as much as I, if I must sell."

"No, she doesn't, for my lady'd buy Fair Meadow out from under you. You'd best stop looking for a buyer and start lookin' for a husband to give you heirs."

"Trent! A husband does not give his wife heirs. That is her duty and privilege."

"Well, you've been sadly neglecting your duty, ma'am." Trent continued to wag her finger, despite Sarah's astonished frown.

Perhaps, Sarah thought ludicrously, her scowl had turned inexplicably upside down. It was the only reason she could think of to explain her maid's outrageous argument.

"You could have your pick from all the officers returnin' from France who'll be squirin' the ladies around London this summer, an' don't I know it, if only you'd . . . "

Sarah coughed to control the errant laughter that tickled

the back of her throat. "You are correct. I have neglected my duty."

Trent, giving an emphatic shake of her head that said "I told you so," prompted Sarah to successfully affect a quelling stare. "My aunt would say I have allowed you to become far too outspoken in your opinion."

Dipping a repentent curtsey, Trent apologised. "I meant no disrespect, Miss. Perhaps I overspoke myself. But Miss, with all this talk of solicitors, I'm worried. What about us? Garner, his family, and myself. Where'll we go, if you sell out? I cannot stand thinkin' of workin' for a different mistress." She buried her nose in a serviceable handkerchief. "There's only one help for us. Go to London . . . "

Incredulously, Sarah exclaimed, "You never give up, do you?" She rose from the table and faced her abigail, cool, grey eyes to watery blue ones and clasped her palms together prayerfully, touching her chin to the tips of manicured fingernails. Then, as though she were laying all her cards upon the table, she spread her hands into an open fan and confessed, "I own I am disappointed not to go. But even if it were proper for me to be mistress of my own establishment in Town, I could not go. Where is the money to pay for rent, a companion, costumes, servants, a job coach and horses?" As she listed the requirements, she ticked them off on her fingers, then demanded, "Do I have a fairy godmother who can with a wave of her hand conjure up these necessities? Do not badger me with romantic plots. I no longer believe in such tales." Deflated by her admission, she sank onto the needlepoint cushion of the side chair.

Trent's lips were tightly compressed as though she were struggling to control her valiant tongue. She picked up the coffee pot and turned towards the kitchen stairs, still pleading her case. "Perhaps you won't be findin' a pot o' gold at the end o' the rainbow. But I'm still for goin'. You won't be catchin' a husband as long as you sit here in Northamptonshire, that's for certain. . . . " The door swung closed on her appeal.

Rather than sit at the table with her unhappy thoughts, Sarah rose and made her way to the morning room which had been converted into a school room. The walls, papered with apple-green silk, were covered with maps and mathematical equations. A Queen Anne writing desk faced the three rows of rough plank benches and tables where, for the last two years, her students—children of the tenants still remaining at Fair Meadow and the more prosperous neighbouring estate, Dunmead—had laboured over sums and spelling.

She studied the tattered schoolroom trimmings. As she came to a map of the Continent, she traced the Allies's hard won route across the Peninsula and the Pyrenees to Paris. A little more than a year ago, her father had fought his way into Vitoria with the then Marquis of Wellington. Not long afterwards, Sarah had received the news that Sir Henry was dead—killed by a duellist's misfired pistol. Thus had begun a year of travail.

Surfeited with unhappy memories, Sarah tore down the map.

"Mith Thara?"

Turning towards the timid voice at the window, Sarah saw the curly red hair of Tabitha Garner, the stableman's youngest daughter. She rolled up the map and went to see what the child wanted. Smiling down at her, Sarah asked, "What is it Tabby?"

"You have a caller." With a grimy finger, the child pointed down the lane. "Thomebody important. Maybe the Earl. He'th home, Mum say." Sarah knew Tabby's mother had been gossiping with Dunmead's cook.

"No, I didn't know, Tabby. Thank you for telling me," Sarah said. Shading her eyes against the morning sun, she glimpsed a closed carriage making its way up the twisting drive, only occasionally visible among the trees. "Are you losing another tooth?"

Nodding, Tabitha blushed, so that her golden freckles were masked. "Thank you, ma'am." She hesitated, then, bringing forth her left hand which she had kept hidden behind her she blurted out, "Thethe are for you!" and thrust a heavy-headed bouquet of roses, the stems wrapped in burlap, towards her idol. Sarah clasped the flowers to her bosom and watched Tabitha escape in a mad dash away from the house before she could voice her gratitude.

Lifting the bouquet to her face, she closed her eyes and inhaled the aromatic sweetness of the blossoms. They were warm from the morning sun, and the balmy essence was like a soporific mist. Silken petals brushing against her cheek and throat elicited in one weary of heavy woolens and scratchy bombazines, the poignant memory of delicate floral-hued gowns of petal-soft fabrics.

Sarah opened her eyes upon the startling realisation that her reverie had waxed sentimental to the point of becoming maudlin. She went to the kitchen, where she arranged the roses herself, then carried the vase to her bed chamber. The servants gossiped about the smallest details and she didn't want Tabby's feelings hurt by the news that her gift had not been treated with respect.

When she came back downstairs she was informed that a gentleman awaited her in the salon. Sarah beamed with anticipation. Tabitha had been right, then; the Earl of Pemberton, was again in the country, having resigned his commission. She hurried into the room.

Upon her entrance, Arthur Quoinby rose from the rusty satin settee and sketched a bow. He extended his right hand as he said, "Good morning," in his usually doleful tones.

Her solicitor's unsummoned appearance stopped Sarah's advance and checked her joy. She stared at him. He had too often been the bringer of bad news. Finally, regretting her lapse of manners, she motioned for him to be seated. She chose a peach-coloured arm chair and said, "I did not expect you, Mr. Quoinby."

The solicitor perched on the edge of the old-fashioned settee. "No, ma'am," he replied as he retrieved a leather pouch from the worn carpet. Unclasping the flap, he fidgeted and cleared his throat, as though unsure how to begin the business.

It was Sarah's experience that the dry-boned solicitor was never slow in delivering bad news. She wondered what could be so terrible as to make it impossible for him to find his voice. "We have some pressing business to discuss," she prompted, hoping to stem the panic that had begun to beat in her throat. When he still did not speak, she offered him refreshment.

"Thank you no," he said, in a thin, reedy voice. Then, smacking his lips, he ventured, "Unless you have spruce beer?"

She rang the bell and made known to Mattie her guest's desire for a glass of Sir Henry's last batch of the pungent brew.

Sarah worried that Mr. Quoinby had discovered yet another creditor with a claim against her father's estate. Reluctant to press him as to his business with her, and equally unwilling to present the matter which plagued her, she watched as he found his spectacles in his waistcoat pocket, and placed them on his nose. He began to leaf through a sheaf of papers, his glowering look and officious shuffling increasing Sarah's dread. She told herself she must not ascribe anything sinister to her solicitor's habitual scowl; it was a consequence of constantly perusing complicated documents. Forcing herself to remain calm, she folded her hands on her grey crape skirt to await the moment when he broached the purpose of his visit.

He was untying the strings of a folder when the maid returned with a tankard, startling Sarah out of her jittery expectancy. She did not fail to see the sidelong glance Mattie cast in her direction and straightened her spine lest her people think their situation at Fair Meadow hopeless.

After quaffing a considerable quantity, Mr. Quoinby sighed. "Ah. The last batch is always the best." Finally, he opened the folder.

Sarah realised she had been holding her breath in unhappy anticipation. When her solicitor took out a letter she released her breath in an audible sigh.

Mr. Quoinby glanced up. "Beg pardon, ma'am?"

Sarah smiled. "How relieved I am to see Lady Pemberton's seal," she confessed. "Now, I can hope you have brought me good news."

As Mr. Quoinby unfolded the letter, he laughed a little. "I am sure it must be. I have never had such difficulty delivering bad news." Still, Sarah was not reassured as he squinted at the cross-written page, pursing his lips in a puzzled grimace. "This is most irregular, ma'am. Her ladyship is issuing you a summons."

For a moment, Sarah did not know quite how to respond. A summons? Lady Pemberton was not usually so commanding. Finally, she shrugged her shoulders in puzzlement. "I should be happy to visit my godmother. She has only to ask; but I was not aware she was at Dunmead."

"She is not in the neighbourhood," said Mr. Quoinby. "She is in London and wishes your company."

Though she was considerably surprised, Sarah disciplined her features. "That would be rather difficult, sir. You see, I received a letter from my aunt this morning requesting that I not come to London."

"Lady Anne?" Placing his spectacles on his forehead, Mr. Quoinby frowned at Sarah as though he were cross-examining a witness.

Nervously, Sarah nodded.

"The Dowager Lady Pemberton outranks your aunt. I believe her wishes must prevail."

"Yes, of course," Sarah agreed. "But I am certain Aunt Anne will not like to see me." Her hands fluttered into nervous flight. With an effort, she reposed them once more on her lap.

Mr. Quoinby set the spectacles on his nose once more. "Lady Pemberton is quite clear in her letter. She writes, 'Miss Fairchild is not to put you off with excuses. I wish to introduce her to those in society who will most effectively advance her hopes.' Hmmm," he said, dabbing at rheumy eyes before squinting again at Sarah. "This does sound like good news."

Sarah was well aware of her godmother's fondness for promoting forlorn hopes. Hadn't she encouraged Sarah's wish to educate the neighbourhood children so they might find employment as clerks and shopkeepers rather than as miners or factory labourers? It was entirely possible, she thought with growing optimism, that her godmother had discovered among her acquaintance someone who would be willing to back a school for young ladies. Sarah could scarcely contain her excitement as she said in a rather shaky voice, "I hope I may be able to repay my godmother's kindness."

From his quizzical look, Sarah surmised that Mr. Quoinby had his doubts about her ambitions. When he spoke, she wondered whether he had been attending. "Excuse me, Miss Fairchild. You may tell me it is none of my business, but it is my opinion that you are in need of some cheerfulness."

Her spine straightened. "I beg your pardon, I thought I heard you say I needed cheerfulness." She arched a blonde eyebrow dubiously. "It seems a change from the usual chorus of 'Economies.' How am I to reconcile the two?"

Mr. Quoinby referred again to the correspondence. Jabbing the paper with his forefinger, he declared, "You need reconcile nothing. Lady Pemberton wishes her 'goddaughter will consider no expense to be borne by herself. I shall provide her complete wardrobe and bear all costs pertaining to her equipage, entertainment, amusement, which I hope will lead to a very promising offer,'" Glancing uneasily at his young client he continued "'of marriage . . .'" His voice trailed off.

Stunned, Sarah came to her feet and paced the length of the room. "She cannot be serious!" she exclaimed, as the solicitor fumbled with his neck-cloth. "I cannot believe my godmother will force me to the altar. It will seriously jeopardise my school. How could I expect parents to entrust their daughters to the care of a newly married bride. Worse, how could I ask a bridegroom to tolerate the impossible moods of giggling schoolgirls? I cannot do it."

"I advise you to accept the Countess's generous offer," Mr. Quoinby replied in a voice that was maddeningly calm. "What harm can it do you to re-enter Society? None, I daresay. Certainly you cannot appear without a proper wardrobe, even if you wish merely to promote your seminary." He shrugged. "Who knows. Perhaps you will also make Lady Pemberton happy."

Sarah examined her neatly darned cuff and caught her lower lip between her teeth. He was right, of course. She could not promote her school in these rags. But to make the rounds of the Marriage Mart at her age. Ludicrous. "Does my godmother name the gentleman who is to tender the offer upon which her hopes depend?"

"My lady says only that she wishes you to marry well and soon." Mr. Quoinby's face darkening, he tugged again at his rumpled starcher.

Sarah turned her back on him, saying with determination, "Very well, Mr. Quoinby, since it would be very poor-spirited in me to refuse, send me to London. Perhaps I shall have the good fortune to win the 'mysterious eligible's' support for my school."

"If you can avoid it, it would be best, Miss Fairchild," he said thoughtfully. "A man may encourage his lady's good works before tying the knot, but you will find most of them keep a tight grip on the pursestrings afterwards."

Understanding the truth of his words, Sarah placed herself once more on the peach-coloured chair. Leaning forwards, she said, "Is my godmother so confident in my marriageability despite my years?"

"Without a doubt, Miss," he replied, smiling kindly.

"I have not given up hope myself," she confessed, as modest colour infused her cheeks. "But I cannot help knowing I am not generally recognised a beauty." She raised her golden eyebrows ingenuously when Mr. Quoinby tutted disagreement. "I assure you ... my nose is too short," turning in profile towards her sympathetic listener. "And I have spots."

"A few freckles, Miss," he corrected.

"Ah, you did notice them," she said, rubbing the tip of her retroussé nose.

He grinned and said, "But they are charming."

"Nevertheless, they are not fashionable." She raised her shoulders in a graceful shrug. "But to be honest, I rather like them."

"Then what do you care whether others judge them ill?" he enquired.

"It seems I am also guilty of thinking too little of what others think," she said. "I have been told I am too wide of mouth for my own good."

"Your honesty can be daunting," he owned with a gentle nod of his balding head. "But you have been in retirement for a year, and know better when to keep your own counsel."

She blushed. "I cannot promise miracles, but we must hope for the best, sir."

"Even though you are no diamond," he prompted. Sarah felt a fleeting sense of disappointment that faded when he continued with an arch smile, "Lady Pemberton informs me she will turn you into one."

"Aunt Anne will not half like this," Sarah said.

"I should think your aunt will be more relieved that she is not to bear the expense of your holiday." Mr. Quoinby folded Lady Pemberton's letter and tucked it within his pouch. Then, finishing his glass of beer, he summoned Trent. She appeared rather too quickly, as though she had been listening from the hallway. "See to your mistress's household affairs, Miss Trent. Lady Pemberton sends a coach for her in three days."

"Three days! But my classes. . . . " Sarah sputtered to a halt.

"Your students will not mind if you cancel the rest of the term," he said.

It was true; the neighbourhood children had spent the last month gazing dreamily out the French windows as they watched spring transform the dreary landscape into verdure. Sarah could imagine their whoops of joy when she made her announcement.

As the maid left the room with an uncharacteristic rustle of her skirts, Arthur Quoinby snapped the pouch closed and came to his feet. "I am not sorry to admit this is the best day's business I have ever been party to. I hope you will bear your godmother's interference gracefully, ma'am, and that I may drink a toast at your wedding."

Sarah accompanied him to the door. "Pray, do not raise your glass prematurely. I do not anticipate an easy conquest." She suddenly waxed serious. "In that event, I think it expedient to solicit a buyer for Fair Meadow." Her voice faltered, but she pressed on, willing herself to remain serenely unaffected by the future. "I will, of course, require a good price from a buyer who is sympathetic to our people."

Mr. Quoinby took her hand, but refrained from his usual jarring shake. "I shall have an appraisal made."

"Whatever you do," Sarah said, clasping his hand beseechingly, "Do it quickly."

She did not see him out, but hurried off to inform her arriving students that today was the last day of school.

2

SEVERAL LARGE PARCELS from Mrs. Bell's arrived soon after Mr. Quoinby took his leave. As Mattie unpacked the boxes, lifting from silver paper wrappings a pelisse of blue striped lutestring, a pink shot silk spencer, four gowns—a blue cashmere carriage dress, a green-striped book muslin promenade dress, a peach silk morning dress, a walking dress of white jaconet, trimmed with pink ribbon—plus silk stockings, kid slippers, gloves and hats to match, and night gowns and underthings, Sarah realised that Lady Pemberton had spared no expense in outfitting her. Though it seemed that her godmother was loading the dice, Sarah was startled to find herself enjoying the game. Excitement tinted her pale cheeks pink and made her grey eyes shine as though she was party to a good joke.

Before she was quite ready, two days had come and gone. The third found Sarah rising early and pacing the floor of her bedroom. Drawing the curtains aside with the eagerness of an excited child, she asked, "Is the coach here yet?" as Trent entered her bedchamber.

The enameled clock on the mantle chimed eight o'clock. "You know it is not to come before ten," he said, requesting Mattie to set the tray on a small pedestal table which sat before the window. "And standin' in front of that open window in your nightgown won't bring it round any sooner." Sarah turned and caught sight of herself in the mirror. Sunlight streaming through the pane shone white through the thin muslin of her nightgown, making her

15

appear clothed in nothing more than light. Trent snatched a new crimson silk wrapper from the foot of Sarah's four poster bed. "Here, Miss, put this on and have your breakfast."

Sarah slipped her arms into the loose sleeves, and impatiently endured Trent's ritual of tying strings and arranging gathers, then returned to the window. "We have fine weather for our journey," she reported. Then, seeing a gentleman walking from the stables, she nervously adjusted the heavy drapery to afford herself a more sheltered view of a tall gentleman who was walking with an aristocratic bearing which was only enhanced by his reliance upon a silver-handled walking stick. "Has Mr. Quoinby sent the appraiser already?" she asked. Her stomach burned anxiously. "I thought he meant to wait until I had gone."

"He's just home from the war," Trent said, as she peered around the drapery. "Probably sold out. Good tailor, either Weston or Schweitzer." Sarah could not deny the well-cut blue riding coat and buckskin breeches which admirably adorned his well-formed frame. The very sight of him seemed to take away her breath, and her capacity to think. Irritated by her untoward response to the sight of a stranger, she dropped the curtain as Trent spoke.

"Maybe this is the end of your war, Miss."

Sarah was beset with second thoughts. How could she sell the home in which she had grown up? Perhaps she ought to offer it to let until . . . She hurried from the window, holding her wrapper closed at her throat as if she were cold. "Oh, Trent, I shan't see him! Send him away. Tell him I've changed my mind!"

"That I will not, for you have not," came the firm answer as Trent drew a chair from the table. "Don't fret yourself, Miss. Have your breakfast. I'll see to the gentleman." Obediently, Sarah seated herself and began the breakfast of coddled eggs, ham, and strawberries in cream while her abigail left the room.

Sarah was finishing her coffee when Trent returned.

Regarding her abigail with apprehension, Sarah asked, "Is he still here?"

"You will wish to speak to this gentleman, Miss."

"Very well." Exasperated by the fears which had beset her, Sarah threw down her napkin and rose from the table. "If you cannot make my wishes known, I shall tell him myself." Skimming the crimson wrapper from her shoulders before Trent could offer her services, she said, "You could at least offer him coffee in the morning room." Her nervousness made her request sound sharper than she meant it. She regretted the tone immediately, but could not apologise as her abigail was closing the door behind her.

She did not hurry her morning toilette, but since her other new clothes had been packed, she dressed in the blue carriage dress and pulled her long hair into a demure chignon at the nape of her neck. When the clock on her mantel was chiming nine o'clock, she was striding belowstairs with a determined step. She discovered her caller, not cooling his heels as she had intended, but already at work, inspecting the molding around the chimneypiece.

Without making her presence known, she appraised him. By the superb cut of his dark blue coat and the extremely high starched neck-cloth, she judged him to be aping the fashions of the members of the Four-in-Hand Club. That the style became him admirably did nothing for her temper or pulse. Contrary to popular opinion, Sarah ascribed to the belief that clothes did not make the man.

"Good morning," she said. Her tone meant business. When he turned in surprise, she put out her hand and continued her cool welcome. "You have wasted your time in coming today. I have changed my mind."

The person accepted her hand and bowed over it. His bow was arrested in mid-sweep as he looked up. "You have? I was given to understand your decision was quite firm." A disarming smile overspread his handsome, dark features.

Sarah was not prepared for an argument, or for his smile. "Yes, well, it is," she stammered, tugging on her fingers. He had not given up her hand. She wanted it back, for she was suffering an agony of self-consciousness that had begun the moment he had clasped her fingers. Or, she amended, had begun while he was passing beneath her window. She dropped her gaze from his warm, brown eyes to their joined hands. "That is, I wish you will come back to tomorrow, after I am gone."

His brow creased slightly in puzzlement. "Where are you going? Did you not say you had changed your mind?"

Under the impression that the impertinent man was about to erupt into laughter, Sarah freed her hand from his grasp, and delivered a quelling look which, judging from his smile, did nothing to dampen his spirits. "I did. What should it matter to you whether you see the house today, or tomorrow?"

"None at all." His smile faded, as though he was momentarily confused, but it quickly returned and his voice lowered attractively. "Except that you are here to show it to me today. I should like that."

"But I should not," she replied. This person was entirely too cavalier in his manner. She must insist Mr. Quoinby send another person to appraise her property. "I have no time . . . I am leaving for London this morning."

"Your post-chaise has not yet arrived," he said perversely. "I suppose you did not mean to walk?"

"Of course not. My godmother is sending her coach for me." Sarah's spine stiffened as she announced, "But really, this is none of your affair, Mr. . . . ?" Her setdown stumbled to a halt as she realised she had not ascertained his name.

"Dash," he volunteered. "I take it I have the honour to be addressing Miss Fairchild." He extended his hand as though that formality had not already been observed.

Without accepting his hand, which she deemed not a formality, but another instance of familiarity, Sarah conceded that she was. She suspicioned that behind those smiling brown eyes that crinkled in the outward corners, he was still laughing at her. She did not take well to dandies such as Mr. Dash for whom everyone afforded amusement.

"I do not like to be rude, Mr. Dash," she said, exceedingly discomfited by his manner of self-confidence, nay arrogance, which to her mind was entirely unbefitting a clerk. And his name was beyond anything respectable. Mr. Dash, hah! "But I find your manner quite too forwards. As Mr. Quoinby's man . . . "

"You mistake me, Miss Fairchild," he interjected haughtily. Placing his weight on his uninjured leg and the expensive walking stick, he affected the posture of one accustomed to command. "I am not Mr. Quoinby's man. Indeed, Miss, I answer to no man."

Taken aback by his peremptory declaration and the well-practiced posturing, Sarah could only say, "Oh." Her gaze fell to the slate-tiled floor as it occurred to her that Mr. Quoinby might have engaged an agent from London to conduct this business. She appreciated the fact that it would greatly benefit her to have the services of one who counted members of the *ton* among his clients, but she could wish that Mr. Dash was not so handsome. Or independent. She became aware of a prolonged and awkward silence and seized upon this point as one which might dispose him more favorably. "Your independence is most admirable, sir."

His brown eyes twinkled. "You do not approve of my independence."

Sarah moistened her lips as she realised that he did not care a fig for her approval. Rather, she was forced to admit, she must court his if she wished him to set a fair price for her home. She attempted to reply in a conciliatory tone. "I am certain my likes will not sway you, sir. Being independent, you will conduct yourself as you are used to." Her speech had not the effect she intended. His grin widened; she was quite at a loss for words, except to ask sharply, "Why are you laughing, Mr. Dash?"

"My dear Miss Fairchild, I feared this trip would be devilish dull; now, I am glad I agreed to make it. You have convinced me that a country miss possesses as much spirit as one bred to town life."

"We are not easily taken in," Sarah said. "Do you wish to see the house now?"

"Only if you agree to be my guide," he said.

"I should be pleased to show you the house," she said as a peace offering. "If you will not mind that I might have to leave in the middle of your tour."

"Not at all," he said, bowing compliance.

She lowered her head, gathering her thoughts. When she raised it, she began a recitation of those points which she felt would insure a large offer for her home. "The original house was built in 1732, with additions of the conservatory and billiard rooms in 1774 and 1797. The morning room, . . . "

He seemed to be paying scant attention to the details which she was so carefully pointing out—the fine plaster and gilt moldings in the morning room, the oval dining room, the floor to ceiling windows in the conservatory. Should she own that attractive but unfortunately expensive feature had cost her a fortune in window taxes? No, she decided, if he knew his business, such an admission must be superfluous.

Why was he staring at her in such a quizzical fashion, she wondered. It was altogether too much like being ogled in Hyde Park, which always put her out of countenance.

"The kitchen is equipped to feed up to two hundred," she stammered, following him down the stone steps. Pausing to moisten her lips, she said, "Would you believe the house was built around a spring?" When he did not reply except with a distracted grumble, she caught her lower lip between her teeth and tried to rally his interest. "Fair Meadow had one of the first—stoves installed in the county."

A frown pulled his dark eyebrows across his forehead.

Mistaking his expression for irritation, Sarah readily admitted. "I am not completely conversant with this part of the house. If you require more information, I am sure Mrs. Garner can supply it."

"Actually, you have supplied me with more information about kitchens than I should ever have need to know," he said. "Perhaps we could see the upper storey?"

Sarah was certain that guiding him through the bed-chambers was not to be done. Even if it were not improper, she was much too aware of Mr. Dash as a man to allow him to see her private suite. Merely the thought infused her cheeks with hot colour. Immediately, she regained her aplomb and declined firmly, but with grace. "I think not. Perhaps you will be so kind as to return after my . . . staff has had the opportunity of airing the rooms which have been closed." Then, moving away from the proprietary hand which had supported her through the morning room, she led the way into the front hall.

Sarah paused before the great oak staircase and glanced upwards. Several pale rectangles outlined the places where portraits had formerly hung. "The paintings had to be sold." She hesitated, then gathering her courage with a deep breath, said, "My father bought his Lieutenant Colonelcy before the Battle of Vitoria, and was killed before he was able to repay his creditor." She wondered why had she made such an embarrassing confession to a stranger.

"I am sorry for that," he said sounding sincere.

Nodding wistfully, she said, "Yes. Well, if the paintings were still here it would increase the price for Fair Meadow." It served no purpose to bemoan their loss. She was going to London. It was best not to look back.

At that moment, she had much to anticipate. Gravel crunched beneath the wheels of the carriage which had come to deliver her to her godmother's home on Curzon Street. "I have to go," she said, holding out her hand in farewell. "Good day, Mr. Dash."

Her breath caught in her throat as his hand engulfed hers, and she forced herself not to pull her nervous fingers away.

Appearing from the back hall, Trent announced, "I have taken the liberty of having your horse brought around, my—"

"Excellent," he interjected, laying a finger aside his mouth. The abigail proffered his hat and driving gloves, then dipped a curtsey and retreated.

Sarah allowed Trent to arrange the folds of her new blue-striped pelisse, while she herself tied the strings of her new bonnet. Turning at last from her reflection to her abigail, she said, "At last, we're off to London! Go take your place in the coach, if you don't mind Trent. I'd like a moment alone in the house."

After the briefest hesitation, Trent nodded, saying, "As you wish, Miss," then carried her employer's portmanteau to the waiting conveyance.

Mr. Dash was still waiting, hat in hand, at the door. Unable to quell the disturbing premonition that her life would be forever changed when she walked through the front door, Sarah said, "Pray, do not let me keep you from your business, sir."

He bowed graciously, then went outside, as though understanding her wish to say farewell to her home. Strolling around the foyer, gazing into silent chambers, Sarah remembered happier times when the rooms had been filled with love and the rafters had rung with laughter. She had slid down the stairs on satin comforters, landing once at her father's feet. Sir Henry had decided his daughter had too much time and too little occupation, and had set to teaching her how to manage the estate. Education had given her an appreciation of her property and her role in preserving it, and, she hoped, the manner of preservation. She would restore love and laughter to her home.

That ambition propelled her outside.

Seeing Trent taking a seat in the heavy coach which was being loaded with baggage, Sarah was startled by the realisation that she was to ride, unaccompanied by her maid, in a curricle. As Mr. Dash handed her up, she supposed that the driver, a squat, solid-looking man who clenched a cold meerschaum between his teeth, had been charged with delivering her into London. She was not half-pleased with the arrangements for her removal to Town.

Mr. Dash was striding to the near side of the yellow-painted curricle. Struck by the dreadful notion that he meant to escort her to London, Sarah began to give voice to protest. To her horror he held out his hand to the driver and said, "If you will take my horse, Nigglesworth . . ." Obligingly the man turned the reins over to the dandy, and strode towards Garner who was reverently holding a black steed which looked too high-blooded to belong to one of Mr. Dash's like. That he thought highly of himself, Sarah had repeatedly seen. She was of the opinion that he needed to be reminded of his place.

As he seated himself at her side and adjusted his hold on the ribands, she finally gave voice to her exasperation. "Mr. Dash! Have you lost your mind?"

Stretching his long legs across the footwell, he was regarding her with the expression of a schoolboy caught in mischief. "I must have," he admitted, looking down at the reins in his hands. "You must forgive me, for taking advantage of our friendship."

She leaned suspiciously away from him and said in her frostiest voice, "You overestimate your appeal, sir. I wish you will step down immediately."

He shook his dark head. "Regretfully, I cannot oblige you. I usually undertake to drive my own curricle."

"Yours? But my godmother was to send her coach for me."

"I know. But since I was in the neighbourhood, I hope you will not look too unkindly upon your neighbour fetching you to London."

"My neighbour?" She regarded him in distrusting confusion. "But my neighbour is the Earl of Pemberton." He was nodding. "I beg your pardon. You are Lord Pemberton? How is it possible that you are . . . Edward . . . Dash?" The Earl's family name was Norris, but she had nicknamed him Dash because he seemed always to be in a hurry. But he looked nothing like her childhood playmate and tormentor. Dash had been fair, with straight, sand-coloured hair that was always tangled. This man was dark; his black hair curled like a ram's fleece over the starched neck-cloth. How could they be one and the same?

Surely, he was gammoning her. His smile certainly led her to believe he was enjoying her discomfiture. Oh, she acknowledged with a finger to her lips, that would be like her old playmate.

Something in the way he was staring at his hands, a half-forgotten memory of chagrin and smoldering resentment finally convinced her. Holding out her hand as if they had just been formally introduced, she proclaimed, "You are Edward. My Lord, welcome home."

With a maddening grin twisting his handsome face, he nodded as he took her hand. An explosive breath escaped her control. "I should think that sort of prank beneath an earl's dignity."

Laughing aloud, Lord Pemberton cracked the whip over the heads of his matched bays. He waited until the clatter of departure had settled into a rhythmical rumble before saying, "I hope you will forgive my masquerade."

For some seconds she was unable to form a rational thought as embarrassment heated her blood. What a nodcock she was to have mistaken the Earl of Pemberton for a common man. But he could have saved her this humiliation if only he'd told her at the outset who he was. "Why did you not tell me?" she demanded, blushing furiously as she decided he had deliberately misled her. "I thought you had come to . . . "

"Buy your house?" he suggested. As they were travelling along a straight stretch of road, he looked at her. Exasperated beyond toleration, she turned her countenance from him.

Returning his attention onto the road, he said, "I hope it will not be necessary for you to sell."

She was embarrassed that he should sham her, then laugh at her gullibility and express sympathy in the same breath. She gave him a sideways look, saying in a subdued tone, "No more than I, my Lord. That is why I go to London.

I have hopes of finding patrons for my school."

His lip quirked knowingly. "No, really? I should never have thought it of you. That stuff," indicating the rich fabric of her pelisse and the latest bonnet, "is not the fashion among school-mistresses."

"No, My Lord." Sarah gazed at the wheat field past which they were speeding on the raised road. Then, "My godmama insists I must look for whatever opportunity will preserve Fair Meadow."

He rubbed his smooth chin thoughtfully. "Meaning the Marriage Mart?" Giving him a polite nod, she was surprised to see his eyebrows raise enquiringly. "You remain unmoved by my mother's ambition?"

Sarah regarded him without blushing, as she confessed, "I am rather embarrassed by it."

"Very becoming modesty," he teased. "That, I am persuaded, is the all go among educationalists. Tell me, whom do you educate?"

Sarah wished he would stop taxing her. Turning cool grey eyes on him she said, "You are laughing at what may possibly be the salvation of my inheritance."

He did not look at her, but attended to the business of driving. "You sell yourself short, if you think a school could save your home. Given the run of the place, boys would destroy it with practical jokes and penknives."

"I am persuaded you speak from experience." An amused smile edged the corners of her mouth, but, hiding it behind the brim of her bonnet, she did not allow him to witness her indulgence.

"That is, I am told, the best teacher," he replied. "However, the real lesson was learned from a birch rod, not from youthful highjinks." She blushed again as she realised he was appraising her slender form. "How did you propose to enforce discipline?"

Aghast, she protested, "I shall certainly not employ a rod, my Lord. Young ladies also need an education."

The Earl attended to a reluctant goer, then asked in an

off-hand tone, "Are you a blue-stocking, Miss Fairchild?"

She did not quite know what to make of his query. Did he, like so many others, condemn intelligent women? And what if he did, she asked herself, squaring her chin. She cared nothing for his approval. "As to that I make no claim, unless wishing to impart genteel knowledge to young ladies who wish to improve their station in life is a qualification."

"I hardly think so," he replied. "But in other circles, your ambition will not be well-received. If you advertise in Society your intention of setting up a school, I cannot think you will meet with success in that Other Matter."

At that moment, the off-side pacer, seeing a threatening movement in the gorse at the edge of the road, swerved in its traces. Lord Pemberton turned his wrist over and snapped the rein against the animal's hind leg in such a way as to encourage it to ignore all but its master's will. Sarah was awed by his adroit handling of a troublesome animal.

"A new husband is unlikely to welcome a gaggle of giggling schoolgirls into his home," he remarked.

Unwilling to own that the same thought had already crossed her mind, she met his sidelong gaze evenly. "Then it is to my advantage to remain single, My Lord."

"I cannot believe it," he said, in a tone which suggested he was out of humour with her quiet assertion. "You owe a great deal which I think cannot be repaid unless you marry well."

In a small voice which she hoped concealed growing anger, Sarah said, "You do not know me, My Lord, yet you tell me what I must do. I know my need, but I am not ready to sell myself to the highest bidder."

"But you would sell your home, your inheritance, and leave yourself nothing to attract an agreeable mate?"

The wind caught the wide brim of Sarah's bonnet and threatened to unseat her. Holding onto her hat, she struggled to retain her dignity. "I take comfort in your honesty," she said ironically. "It must be my one consolation, I suppose."

Shrugging, Lord Pemberton ceded, "I was perhaps too blunt, but I am concerned that you wish to discard your ace. You cannot deny that Fair Meadow is an enviable dowry. It goes a long way in off-setting the disadvantage of debts."

Sarah shot dagger looks at him. His estimation made her feel like an old shoe. Still, she was not so animadverted by his outspoken concern that she was unable to reply with humour. "Thank you, My Lord. Your description of my allure makes me tremble lest I find myself at my last prayers. Nevertheless, it does stiffen my resolve to educate other girls."

He was compelled to attend to the crossing of a narrow bridge from which his horses seemed to shy. Relaxing in the silence of birdsong and the clatter of iron against pavement, Sarah recruited her strength, as it became apparent that his lordship's interest in their discussion had waned.

Suddenly he shattered her complaisance. "I wouldn't wager a groat on your school."

Disregarding the moving vehicle, she stood up and said, "If I were a man, you should not speak so to me."

Before she was thrown into a ditch, he pulled her down beside him. "Perhaps not. But if you were a man, I would not concern myself with you." Her mouth pursing indignantly caused him to chuckle. "Now I can believe you are a teacher. I remember that sour expression from my days at Eton." Snapping his whip at a fly in the air, he asserted, "I say it is useless to fill a schoolgirl's head with educational nonsense. The only thing she wants to learn is how to make a wealthy and noble gentleman fall in love with her."

"Nonsense?" she demanded. "Is that what I preach?" She was not gratified to see his emphatic nod. His honesty was more hurtful than any ruse or prank he might have played. She took a deep, controlling breath, releasing it on, "Thank you again, for pointing out the futility of my hopes." At *Pointe Non Plus*, Sarah discovered tears quivering on her lashes. Angrily, she dashed them away. She hadn't cried when Dash had locked her in the grain box to keep her from tagging after him and his chums; she would not cry now. Quietly, she confessed, "When you left Dunmead, I hoped I should never see you again. Now I wish you had not come back."

"I cannot say I am sorry I could not oblige you," he said, slowing the pace of his trotters. "But cheer up. I might engage the wrath of a crack shot who will satisfy your wish on the field of honour."

Sarah's visage went white. She could not believe him that cruel. "I can only assume by that remark that you did not know my father was killed by a duellist."

"No?" marvelled the Earl. "I thought Sir Henry possessed a cooler head than that."

Bristling in defence of her father's reputation, Sarah declared, "My father was no coward, My Lord. Neither was he a fool."

"Touché, Miss. Am I to presume you think I have not changed since I was ten?"

"Your outward appearance has altered, My Lord. That is why I failed to recognise you." Though the Earl had many times been in the thick of battle, and had suffered an injury which seemed to cause him nominal discomfort, Sarah readily admitted that Time had been kind to him. She shrugged. "I suppose you must be acknowledged to be quite handsome." However, pleasing outward appearances masked an inner man of whom she could not approve. "But I cannot think the years have changed you to the good."

"I am sorry to have reinforced your poor opinion of me," he said, as though regretting his pretense. "Once we were friends."

"A very long time ago," she agreed. "But then you wished to impress cousins come to visit for the holidays, and had no sympathy for a child of seven who was afraid of the dark. I didn't like you at all, and was glad your father sent you away to school. I suppose he would have done so in any event, but at the time I thought it was because I asked him."

In a rare moment of forgetfulness, the Earl's watchful gaze left the road. He stared at her. "I beg your pardon?"

At that moment, in front of them, a hay wagon lumbered across the road. Sarah pointed out the peril and exclaimed, "My Lord, look!"

The Earl already had sized up their situation. He sawed on the reins, but the team had the bits between their teeth and their pace barely slowed. While his companion covered her face with a gloved hand, he steered between the tailgate of the obstacle and the marker which proclaimed them sixty-five miles from London.

Lord Pemberton was generally acknowledged as a top-sawyer, but the curricle's speed and the heedless obstruction proved too much even for his skill. The off-side wheel slipped from the packed road surface, missed the mileage post by inches, and bounced over a series of ruts that propelled the curricle further into a ditch alongside the road. Sarah expected at any moment to be hurled into a briar hedge or crushed beneath the wheels.

The Earl managed to slow the bays which seemed to be making an attempt to outrun their burden. But a wheel struck a large, protruding stone and with a resounding crack, a spoke snapped. Several more spokes collapsed while the driver set his team on its haunches to prevent their being overturned.

The curricle sagged on its injured wheel and came to a precipitate halt. Sarah, not being of one piece with the vehicle, began an unexpected flight over the broken-down wheel. Then, landing abruptly on the soft, soggy bottom of the trench, she had the wind knocked out of her. Though it was not in her nature to react in such a missish way, she very nearly sank into a dead faint.

After hastily tying off the reins, Lord Pemberton scrambled out of the conveyance. "Are you hurt?" he demanded, as he worked her limbs to detect broken bones. When she failed to answer, but only gasped, his grip gentled and he tilted her chin so he might look into her eyes, asking, "Sarah? Are you all right?"

"I'm fine," she finally croaked. "Thank you, sir." Suddenly she realised he was kneeling in the mud. "Pray, get up, you are ruining your trousers!" she exclaimed breathlessly, as she attempted to remove herself from his solicitous embrace and stand herself.

"Don't fly into the boughs, Sarah," he teased. When his gentle rejoinder failed to quiet her, his tone became more strident. "Sarah, don't!" His hand tightened at her waist. "You may have suffered a concussion or broken something."

The urgent tone of his voice halted her struggle. She brought her gaze upwards to stare into the face which was separated by less than a handsbreadth from her own. In the shadow cast by the brim of her bonnet, his eyes had darkened. His whispered "Sarah" cooled her cheeks, yet fanned an ember within which she had not known existed, for it provoked her heart into an erratic rhythm which was as rapturous as it was unexpected.

Startled by the beginnings of romantic palpitations, she preferred to attribute her rattling pulse to the fall and not his embrace. The latter possibility she was obliged to consider, however, because of the unbidden sensations which the sound of her name upon his lips had aroused in her. Thoroughly confused by her reaction, she covered his lips with a muddy glove and declaimed in a shaking voice, "I promise I am not hurt, my lord. It is not necessary to kiss me."

"That is good news. And so prettily said," he responded with laughter as he assisted her to her feet. Then, applying a handkerchief to his mouth and to her fingers, "I wish you will stop addressing me as your 'Lord.'"

She took the linen square before he might address the stains on her pelisse. "Would you prefer I call you Mr. Dash?"

"I would prefer to dispense with formality and with nonsense." Refolding his handkerchief, he confessed, "My

Christian name has grown rusty from disuse."

"Edward?" She found pleasure in the syllables and in the fact that it made him smile. Others may tell her she should not encourage him, but she returned a shy smile. "I thought you were a first-rate fiddler."

He returned her gentle taunt with the unvarnished truth. "I am. A cub would have killed you." Dusting off his breeches, he reassured her, "You are safe with me."

Glancing at the stone milepost which stood untouched only a few feet from where the curricle reposed, Sarah swallowed tensely as she realised how close she had come to serious injury. "I do thank you," she said, lifting a grateful smile, and observing how he puffed his chest when she laid her hand in his. His pride piqued her sense of humour. "For not killing me, but merely stranding us in the hot sun."

"We are not stranded," he asserted. "When we have two undamaged mounts. Here, stand aside."

When he attempted to set her in the shade out of the dust and harm's way, she remonstrated, "For heaven's sake, I am no helpless female, who cannot be of use in an emergency. Let me hold the horses while you unhitch them." When he looked doubtfully at her, she went on. "Don't stare, sir. I have handled high-blooded cattle." To prove her point, she moved decisively to the head of the nearest horse. When she caught its bridle, the animal nudged her shoulder and quieted. In a trice, she caught its team-mate's bridle and tried to ignore that one's ill-mannered offer to eat her bonnet.

The Earl had the pair out of harness by the time his groom, riding the black, caught up with them. Upon seeing the derelict curricle, the man dismounted from his lordship's impatient charger, voicing hearty congratulations that neither occupant of the vehicle had been injured.

"Thank you, Nigglesworth," said Lord Pemberton, handing the team's reins to his man. "Be so good as to stable these wretched creatures at the George in Huntingdon. We shall decide what is to be done after refreshing ourselves there." As Nigglesworth hauled himself onto the back of the bonnet-munching bay, the Earl lifted Sarah onto Thundercloud's back, then mounted the restive black himself and set the animal into a comfortable canter.

"My lord . . . Edward," Sarah protested, revising the form of address when she perceived the tight set of his jaw. "Why did you not allow me to ride one of your other horses?"

"I cannot allow you to ride such an animal after the fall you took," he said.

She could accept that excuse, but riding double was extremely uncomfortable. "Perhaps you might ride ahead and send a cart for me."

"Abandon you? What an ogre I must appear to you," he replied. "Are you afraid of me, Sarah?"

"Not at all," she said quickly. "I do not mind in the least waiting. It is only, I am not used to riding. And only think, sir; how does this appear?"

He drew her more securely within his protective embrace. "That I am a chivalrous knight rescuing a damsel in distress."

3

NEVER IN HER life had she been compared to a distressed damsel. Sarah would have laughed at the romantic exaggeration, except that the arm circled protectively around her waist so agitated her that she was unable to form a civil reply. Rather breathlessly, she snapped, "Sir Galahad you are not!"

Edward leaned back his head and laughed aloud. "A hit! By George she can fence. Fortunately, no vital spot suffered from the thrust. Only my pride."

Pleased that her risposte had proven so effective, Sarah affected a compassionate moue and sighed, "Poor, broken man." Mischief again twinkled in her bright eyes. "It is, I fear, a mortal wound."

"A goner, she says," he responded in mock alarm. "When I am in my grave, will you weep for me?"

Sarah felt as though cold fingers played her spine. Shivering, she begged, "Don't, My Lord, I do not wish harm to befall you." She heaved a sigh of frustration. "Oh, why will you not set me down?"

"What is this?" he enquired sharply. "Do you wish to be rid of me?"

Sarah shook her head. "No, My Lord. I would have been satisfied to ride with Trent. It would have saved us both trouble."

"You would have been laughed off the road," he declared. "And I would have been denied the privilege of sparring with a spitfire. So I'll hear no more about abandoning you along the road to travel with your maid."

She was extremely dismayed as it occurred to her that she hardly knew this man, yet was utterly within his power as he carried her before him so forcefully. The experience must have transported a more romantically-minded female into an ecstatic swoon. Sarah was not such a goose as to go limp on horseback; however, the Earl's grip was breathtaking, and she discovered to her chagrin that she was growing dizzy. "My Lord, pray, slow your horse," she demanded with a tug on his rein hand.

Her protest only succeeded in fretting their mount and won her a reprimand from its rider. "Will you sit still, ma'am!" Pemberton demanded. "Or must I carry you over the saddlebow?"

Immediately her struggles ceased, as did her sense of helplessness. Straightening her spine, she presented him a cold shoulder as she challenged, "You wouldn't dare!"

He chuckled again. "Don't be too sure of that. I have attempted it upon occasion and found it the most effective method of rescue."

She choked on a affronted gasp, then said, "I can only hope you are speaking in jest, sir, but I must inform you I do not find your sense of humour at all amusing."

"How black you paint me, Miss Fairchild," he said in a contrite tone. She did not deign to look at him, but occupied herself by gazing across the verdant fields. "What did I do to fall out of your good graces?"

"Nothing," she dissembled nervously. "I don't remember. Please, My Lord, it does not signify." Contrary to her defiant words, it very much did matter. If it did not, why were her hands within their kid gloves, suddenly gone cold? She felt at odds with herself, and very insecure despite the arm settled so comfortably around her.

As they neared the inn, she hoped they could slip into the yard of the George without attracting notice. But that hope died as they drew into that hostel's gates in the dust of the York Highflyer. The coachman's blast on his yard of tin emptied the establishment of all who hoped to profit from the coach's business or find room on the already crowded flying machine.

Accustomed as she was to the peaceful operation of her isolated estate, the bustle in the yard unsettled her even more. The landlord who separated himself from the crowd approached them, did nothing to soothe her uneasiness. His eyes were shifting suspiciously between herself and her escort, but he greeted them courteously enough. "Ah, good afternoon, my lord, my lady. Did you meet wi' a spot of bad luck on the road?"

The Earl dismounted and lifted her to the ground. After her giddy ride, she felt as though she were standing on pins and needles and was irritatingly unable to support herself. She was obliged to cling to her escort's arm until the circulation in her legs resumed.

"Curricle lost a wheel five miles down the road," he said, dispassionately. "Have you a room for the lady? I fear she is not quite the thing."

Sarah tried to affect a more sophisticated appearance, but could tell that she had failed from the landlord's raised eyebrows. He sniffed. "Well, come this way. Ned!" he called, attracting the attention of a gape-mouthed groom who shuffled towards the trio. "Bait the gentleman's horse, lad!" As the youngster took the black's reins, Sarah, on the Earl's arm followed their host past the milling throng of coach-passengers, into the cool interior of his establishment.

Surprised to find herself shaking after all danger was past, Sarah leaned heavily on the Earl's arm. She was aware of a speculative buzz which seemed to follow in their wake. She willed herself to walk on her own two feet so as to still the wagging tongues. She reached the coffee room and gratefully sat in the nearest chair.

"We shall refresh ourselves," Pemberton said. "How does lemonade sound?" When she nodded her thanks, he quickly dispatched the landlord for two glasses, then sat at the table beside her. Rubbing her hands, he commanded gently, "You will not faint."

"I shall certainly not faint, My Lord," she said with spirit as she took her hands back. A blush overspread her pale cheeks as she tried to explain her weakness. "I am not used to riding." She removed her bonnet, and was at once sorry she had done so. Bursting into laughter, she exclaimed, "Your miserable animal ate my hat!"

Bedraggled feathers drooped over a hole in the crown. Sarah poked her hand through the ruined bonnet. "Why did you not say something?" She did not give him the opportunity of answering, but went on giddily. "No wonder our host seems so scandalized. It must appear as though I fell on my head."

At that moment, the landlord produced their lemonade. From the sidelong stares he was casting in her direction, Sarah was certain he thought her a candidate for Bedlam. Worse, he treated her as though she were invisible. But when he enquired in an oily tone implying everything impure about their havey-cavey travelling arrangements, "How long will the lady be needing 'er room, My Lord?" she realised he had taken her not for a Bedlamite, but a ladybird. She was about to correct his mistaken and extremely insulting notion when the Earl drawled in a lazy tone, "My cousin's abigail is following in the coach with the baggage." Sarah glared at him for the invention. Cousin indeed! Had he not learned his lesson from this morning? Her sour expression was rewarded with a puckish grin that seemed as apologetic as it was beguiling.

"However," Edward continued. "She cannot travel in such a lumbersome conveyance. We will be needing a post chaise and four to conduct us to Town."

She observed the landlord as he seemed to be deciding whether or not their patronage would serve him well or ill. She presumed he had decided in their favour, because he ventured, "S'sixty miles t' London, My Lord; and a gruelling trip it'd be if you started out after nuncheon." He was bowing and scraping as though no abasement were too humiliating to bear if it might appease wealthy guests.

Sarah was repulsed and would have demanded the coach immediately, but Edward seemed to be in a more tolerant mood, even when the odious host winked conspiratorially and said, "Will ye require the use of a private parlour for your meals?"

"I think not," Edward replied. Sarah wondered what he must be thinking to suggest that she subject herself to the leers of every Tom, Dick and Harry who chanced to drop into the common room. He had sunk himself beneath reproach in her esteem and so she would tell him, when their oily host withdrew.

She caught the apologetic gleam in the Earl's eye, but she would not be so easily appeased this time. She stared cold daggers at him, hoping to convey her utmost displeasure. His good-humoured grin did not fade beneath her withering stare. Instead, he seemed to feel constrained to enlarge upon his hoax. "My cousin rather fancies having an Adventure before she retires to her country estate in the fall." Wondering whether he had lost all his senses, she darkened her frown. But his grin only widened as if to say "trust me." He was continuing, "I should think dining in public might suit her whimsy."

"Very good, My Lord," responded their host. His manner unbent immediately, as though he saw them in a different and entirely virtuous light. Effusively, he assured them, "I shall have my wife show your cousin to her room."

"What, no baggage?" exclaimed the landlord's missus when she had thrown open the casement window in the best bedchamber she had to offer. She folded her hands prudishly before her starched apron and whined disapprovingly, "Begging your ladyship's pardon, but I run a respectable establishment. . . . "

"And I'm very grateful that you do," said Sarah, placing her ruined bonnet onto the sturdy chest. Although she could not approve of the deception Edward had concocted, she drew a breath and willingly embellished it. "My cousin insisted you would quite understand my reticence at patronising an inn. I have never done such an unladylike thing in my life. But there was nothing else to do, unless I wished to camp out like a gypsy. And you see, I could not bring myself to . . . "

"Well of course not," agreed the wife, removing the mud-smirched pelisse from Sarah's shoulders in a manner which satisfied Sarah that her reputation was safe. "I'm sure you must not have done such a dangerous thing. Now, I'll clean and press this, Miss . . . "

"Fairchild," Sarah replied as she moved to the open window to watch for Trent and the baggage coach.

" . . . Miss Fairchild. You rest for an hour and I'll set out your nuncheon in a corner of the coffee room where you can watch the world without making a spectacle of yourself." So saying, she let herself out the door, when, Sarah had no doubt, she would head for the kitchen to compare notes with her husband.

Having been assured by the landlord that it was no trouble to stable the team or to send men to take the curricle to the wheelwright's shop, Lord Pemberton accompanied his groom into the taproom and ordered two mugs of heavy wet. "I know I can rely upon your discretion," he said while Nigglesworth was imbibing deeply.

"O'course, My Lord," Nigglesworth replied. "I hope the lady didn't suffer a lasting hurt."

Under cover of a burst of laughter at the next table, the Earl said, "My cousin is resting comfortably, thank you. I'll tell Miss Fairchild you enquired about her."

"As you wish, My Lord," the groom said imperturbably. "Shall I hire a post chaise for you and your 'cousin'?"

"Yes, with four horses. We shall leave tomorrow morning accompanied by Sarah's abigail. I should appreciate it if you'd see to my horses and the repair of my curricle. Then, bring Thundercloud to London as quickly as you can."

"As you say, My Lord," said Nigglesworth agreeably. Then, downing his stout, he caught the last drop on his thumbnail, and set the empty tankard on the table. When Edward offered to stand for another, he insisted, "No, thankee, sir; I've got t' get t' work." So saying, he took his feet and made for the stables.

As promised, luncheon—consisting of cold sliced meats, vegetables, cakes, tarts and jellies—was waiting an hour later, in the coffee room. Sarah was relieved to find upon descending the stairs, that except for herself and her new found cousin, the room was empty of customers. Huntingdon was entirely too close to home for her to be comfortable in the familial masquerade the Earl had devised to quell the suspicions of the inn's proprietor. She felt some one of their acquaintance must surely burst through the door and cry shame at their Banbury tale. That, she realised, must put a period to all her hopes.

Thus, with occasional nervous glances at the door, she attacked her meal with more pluck than appetite. She hadn't done anything so daring since she was a child. Aunt Anne would say it was brass-faced of her. But she had to confess, as she accepted a second helping of asparagus from the dour-faced waiter who hovered at her elbow, she'd done nothing so much fun either. Regardless of the outcome of her summer in London, she must look back upon this journey as the highlight of her single life.

Helping himself to a slice of turkey and the dish of asparagus, Edward said affably, "You look exactly like a snared pigeon trying to take flight."

Sarah tossed her golden head and put the lie to his accusation. "That, my dear cousin, was the shadow of my former self. Actually, I was congratulating myself upon the commencement of my Adventure. Shall we do something terribly shocking after nuncheon?"

"In coming here, we already have," he replied, not at all in a teasing voice as his gaze was arrested by an unwelcome sight at the door.

Sarah turned to see what had so diverted her companion's

attention and immediately apprehended they were in a devil of a hank. In a six-caped driving coat, a golden-haired Corinthian filled the door. Upon seeing the solitary couple, his disdainful frown which gave him the appearance of being a deep one, dissolved into a thin-lipped smile of recognition, and he strode forwards in a manner that flared out the capes to make his shoulders appear even broader. "What luck!" he called out.

Muttering something unintelligible to Sarah's ears, Pemberton rose and, offering his hand, said, "Hello, Repton. Last person I expected to see here."

After he gave his coat and York gloves to the waiter, Mr. Repton received Edward's hand in his all the while Sarah's gaze was ensnared by a pair of blue eyes the colour of an October sky. She had been isolated far too long, but she recognised the spark of intrigue which ignited as he held her gaze. At last she lowered her lashes, embarrassed for having stared at him so openly. He went on as though their silent exchange had affected him not at all. "Yes, and I see how you welcome my appearance, M'Lord. But now that I have broken upon your tryst, we might as well make the best of it."

"Have it all wrong as usual, Rep," Pemberton said, placing his hand on the table between Sarah and the intruder. "My cousin, Miss Fairchild."

"I am charmed," Mr. Repton said smoothly.

Sarah was about to offer her hand but found that the Earl was grasping it tightly. She directed a puzzled look at him. "I shall have no adventure, Edward, if you mean to protect me so violently," she said with a teasing smile. "Don't be such a surly boots; introduce your friend."

"I shall regret I ever did so," Edward said, though he did slacken his hold on her hand. "Sarah, Mr. Charles Repton, late of the Coldstream Guards."

Sarah placed her hand in Repton's as he said, "'Late' is nearly correct, Miss Fairchild. When I was injured at San Sebastian, I decided to make an end of that career."

"You were wounded?" Sarah could not help exclaiming. He was the most perfect individual she had ever seen; she could see no evidence of injury.

"Alas, yes," he replied. "But it does not bear talking; I am fully recovered."

"Thank heaven," she breathed.

"I thought you meant to stay in the army," said Edward, re-seating himself and casually leaning his chair on two legs.

"That was my intention," replied Mr. Repton as he reached into a pocket and withdrew a wedge lob.

Sarah found herself a curious witness to his single-handed snuff-taking performance. Flicking open the box with his thumb, he took a pinch and replaced the container with a flourish that, she was sure, never failed to awe those unacquainted with the finér techniques of the art. She acknowledged his prowess with a mildly amused smile.

He continued his tale. "However I came into an inheritance; and rather than let my dependable brother profit from my early death, which if I was to stay with the Guards must surely come to pass, I sold out."

"I'll wager your C.O. had something to say about that," Edward said. He indicated an empty chair at their table. "Seat yourself, Rep, there's enough for the Regent himself."

Mr. Repton accepted the offer. A plate being fetched immediately, he began to fill it. "Nothing I could repeat in polite company." Flashing a smile onto Sarah, he enquired, "Tell me, Miss Fairchild, are you for London?"

"Yes," Sarah replied, carefully avoiding his mocking stare. Despite his physical perfection and angelic countenance, she was not comfortable with him. He seemed entirely too calculating—always measuring the benefits of one action over another. She suspected he was deciding how advantageous an acquaintance with her might be. It was in her best interest she thought to keep him at a distance, but realising they must be thrust together at various affairs this summer, she fortified herself with a deep breath and told him her direction. "Edward is delivering me to my godmother's home."

"Aunt's," Edward corrected, then drew an asparagus tip from his fork.

"Well, which is she?" Mr. Repton leaned his elbows on the table as though he were intrigued by their dispute.

"Edward's mother is my godmother," Sarah answered, letting Mr. Repton make his own conclusion. Then, seeing the Earl bristle like a dog in a manger, she added in a teasing tone, "I think my cousin is jealous."

"So should I be, if you were my relative," Mr. Repton said. "I count myself fortunate that you are not. Perhaps you will allow me to pay my respects in Town."

"You know where I live," Edward grumbled. "I cannot stop you coming round."

"Don't be so disobliging, Edward," Sarah warned in a honeyed voice. Smiling, she begged pardon. "I'm afraid my cousin takes his responsibility towards me entirely too seriously. He's consigned me to my estate after the summer, and I think he means to make certain I go alone."

"Reprehensible." Mr. Repton's nostrils flared, then flashing a smile whose charm was not lost upon Sarah, continued in a lighter vein. "You must have another scheme in mind."

"Rather," Edward said, to her irritation. Did he think he must protect her from everyone? "My cousin means to turn her home into a school."

Lifting his glass, Mr. Repton peered at Sarah through it, as though she were a species of female unfamiliar to himself. "A school?" he queried. Dropping the glass on its cord, he declared, "No, I cannot see it, Miss Fairchild. You have too much the look of laughter about you to be a pedagogue. I smell a hoax."

Sarah could not quell the instinctive gasp which escaped her lips following Mr. Repton's nonchalant declaration.

Pemberton quickly interjected, "I assure you, Rep, it is no hoax. Sarah can affect the most quelling scowl." He shuddered, making Sarah blush at the memory. "It is positively frightening."

"That," Mr. Repton responded firmly, wagging his fork from side to side before setting it on the edge of his plate, "I will not allow."

Unconcerned with Mr. Repton's opinion, Sarah lifted a forkful of sponge cake to her mouth.

"You have concocted this Canterbury tale about your cousin and her school to throw me off the trail of a secret engagement."

"What?" Sarah gasped, as she inhaled a crumb of the cake. Dropping her fork, she looked to the Earl for help. He was unperturbably flicking a dust mote from the otherwise spotless shoulder of his coat. Mr. Repton obligingly struck her between the shoulderblades.

Pemberton said, "You are quite wide of the mark, old friend. There is no engagement. Sarah is quite settled into her single state, though it is my opinion she should induce a wealthy gentleman to propose. By all means," he said, directing a challenging look at his old schoolmate. "Come to Curzon Street. I should be pleased to welcome you into the family."

Mr. Repton's *sang-froid* seemed to slip in the face of the Earl's invitation. However, he made no protest, but merely turned his wrist convulsively, saying, "Very kind," and looking around the empty room as though searching for a way to decline without insulting the lady and earning himself an appointment in Hyde Park.

At that moment, a diminutive tiger in yellow livery entered the coffee room with Mr. Repton's driving coat folded over his arm. He pushed away from the table, promising, "I shall present my card in Curzon Street, My Lord. Your servant, Miss Fairchild."

"Mr. Repton," Sarah responded, very near laughter. "I hope you will not feel obliged to accept Edward's invitation."

"But I am obliged," he assured her, bowing gallantly over her hand as she came to her feet. "And perfectly willing to steal your affection from Dash."

Sarah withdrew her hand, saying in a cool voice, "My affection cannot be stolen, Mr. Repton. Good day, sir." With a final smile at their guest, Sarah took the Earl's arm and allowed him to guide her out of the coffee room and towards the stairs.

Within a quarter of an hour Sarah rejoined her companion, as she had expressed a wish to see the bridge over the River Ouse. On the way, they passed several small shops, but found nothing in the windows to tempt their purses except a blue silk parasol with white satin fringe which Edward insisted upon buying lest the sun burn Sarah's complexion. That bit of business concluded, they proceeded down the street towards the river.

The Ouse flowing lazily beneath stone arches formed a watery mirror of the mediaeval bridge and buildings whose foundations stood at the water's edge. A cloud drifted across the surface of the water beneath the bridge. "How pretty!" Sarah exclaimed as she peered over the rampart. "Much nicer than any watercolour I've done."

"I'm sure you underestimate your skill." Grinning, Edward leaned an elbow on the bulwark.

Sarah returned his indulgent smile and replied, "Please sir, do not add flattery to your faults. My small talent cannot compare with the Master's brush." She raised her brows enquiringly as his smile dissolved. "I beg your pardon; my aunt has repeatedly warned me of the effects of my outspoken tongue."

"Do not trouble yourself on my account," he said. "I am only concerned about Repton's tongue." He tossed a pair of stones into the water below. "We cannot ignore the gossip he will initiate."

Sarah watched the circular ripples distort the reflexions on the water's surface. She realised gossip spread, like the ripples on the water's surface, distorting and disquieting the lives of those who were its subject. But she could see no reason to anticipate the worst. Turning an enquiring gaze upon her escort, she asked, "Do you think so?" His imagination fascinated her, but she could not share his concern. "I'm sure nothing will kill a lie quicker than to ignore it."

"Nothing will kill a lie but to make it the truth," he said emphatically. "We must be engaged."

"For shame, My Lord. You must care more than I, what Society thinks," Sarah replied, negligently turning her back on the wavering reflexions passing below them.

"For myself, not a fig," he claimed as he leaned both elbows on the wall. "But you cannot deny the damage gossip can do you."

She linked her hand through the crook in his arm and allowed him to direct their steps towards the George. "In this instance you are mistaken, My Lord. The World will think our attachment beyond belief. I am at my last prayers; who should expect you, a prize matrimonial catch, to sacrifice yourself." She twirled her parasol, and asserted, "You can have no wish to be leg-shackled merely to validate tittle-tattle." The slight flush which coloured his ears confirmed her suspicions and made her smile.

The Earl enquired in a somewhat disappointed tone, "Do you hate the thought of being my fiancée?"

Squeezing his arm reassuringly, she replied, "You are a prince among men, Edward, and everything in appearance and station that a lady might hope for in a husband." Handsome and of high rank though he was, Sarah preferred an honest man. Unaccountably, however, even she was drawn to him like steel to a magnet. Still, she did not trust her feelings as they concerned him, especially as she knew nothing of his feelings for her. He had neglected to speak of affection, or honour, but only mentioned scandal and gossip. While she claimed no fondness for "romance," she was offended and hurt by his omission. Disappointment and indignation flared into an uninhibited refusal. "But your offer leaves everything to be desired. It is merely another masquerade." She longed to say more, but as they were on a public thoroughfare where everyone and his cousin might hear, she quietly concluded her setdown. "I cannot accept, My Lord, for I am persuaded I do not love you."

= 4 =

LORD PEMBERTON SHRUGGED as if rolling the weight of her refusal from his shoulders. But Sarah knew her answer had startled him, for his mouth opened and closed several times before he replied, "I am not of the opinion that love has anything to do with marriage. It is merely a matter of," a long hand fluttered tantalisingly, " . . . Convenience."

"Am I to understand you consider the choice of one's life companion a matter of convenience?"

"Not as a general rule," he replied. "But there is the matter of Fair Meadow to consider. You need to make an advantageous match. I am willing to ensure your future."

The Earl sounded as though he were a sacrificial lamb being led to the altar! Pemberton was nothing more than a pompous, self-righteous coxcomb! Doubtless, she was supposed to feel an upswelling of gratitude in her heart for his generosity. She was suffused with warmth, she fumed inwardly, not realising that her cheeks had turned bright pink, as her temper flared. "Your too-flattering offer quite takes my breath away," she said, clenching the ivory handle of her sunshade with both hands to keep from slapping his sanctimonious face. Stepping resolutely into the street, she declared, "I am not so desperate as you make me."

"No?" he queried, yanking her from the brink of danger as a draywagon rumbled past them. He held her firmly when she would have jerked free. She felt the thud of his pulse against her arm and wondered whether he felt the agitated thrum of her own heart. Why did he not let her go? Hadn't he humiliated her enough? Evidently he thought he had not brought her low enough, for he continued, "It is written in your face."

She whirled to glare fury at him. She could not help her age. Hot with embarrassment, she took a calming breath to control her rising temper and managed to say in a deceptively cool voice, "As you say, My Lord, I am past my prime. Pray, forgive my outspoken refusal. I meant no offence." The humble reply made her cheeks burn when her inclination was to deliver a stinging rejoinder. Before she did, however, she recollected she was a lady, whose training made it possible for her to keep a light tone. "Indeed, I did not think you meant me to take you seriously."

"The deuce you say. Few ladies in your position would dare to turn down an offer because they doubted its sincerity."

Turning aside, she blinked away angry tears. She would not give him the satisfaction of knowing he had scored a hit. The future loomed before her as forbidding question marks—. What if no one supported her school? Who did she think she was to turn down an earl?

She sniffed disdain at the condemnatory queries and compelled herself to meet Pemberton's skeptical gaze, unwavering as she replied, "I wish you will not pity me for my single state, sir. It is infinitely preferable to a miserable marriage."

A dark eyebrow arched superciliously as though he doubted not only her sincerity, but also her sanity. "What is your game?"

Sarah could not believe her ears. How did he accuse her of playing games? He had hoaxed her, forced her to pitch gammon to honest folk, and asked her to take in the Polite World with a false engagement. Laying a shaking hand on her bosom she demanded, "Do you charge me with playing deep?"

He put her to the blush by sweeping her form with a mocking stare, then replied testily, "No. But you must own, for all your protests to the contrary, your appearance is one of a female making a last-ditch effort to be married."

"Thank you, My Lord" she said warmly. "You have such an accomodating style, I must be mad to turn you down."

The street being clear, he guided her across it forcefully, then mocked her. "Surely I cannot be so mistaken as to suspect you of being mad."

"Nevertheless, you have mistaken me, for thinking I should give my hand simply where it is . . . convenient." She shook off his supporting arm, loathe to admit to herself the advantages of joining their neighbouring estates. Once, she might have welcomed his proposal. Now, she was sorry for it, and thought nothing could induce her to marry Lord Pemberton, even if it meant she must lose her estate. "I want no part of your convenient marriage, My Lord."

"Well, what do you want?" he asked in a peevish tone, as he kicked a stone down the road.

She watched the pebble bounce along the cobbles. As it skidded down the street, she shrugged candidly and said, "Love."

Edward dropped his hand from her elbow. "Bravely spoken," he acknowledged with a sagacious nod. "But exceedingly naive. Love is a dangerously volatile emotion, courted by romantic fools who mistake the throes of adoration and passion with the comforts of respect and reliability."

"I had not taken you for such a pedant," she replied. Fast losing her temper, she retained sufficient control of herself to add, "What you describe, My Lord, is duty. A poor substitute for affection." Then, having safely traversed the thoroughfare and arrived at the George, she snapped her parasol shut. "Our walk has been . . . surprising and instructive. I cannot own, however, that I appreciated the lesson."

"Perhaps in time you will," he said. His disgruntled suggestion brought her to a stumbling halt. He was quick to arrest her fall.

Sarah found herself supported again in strong arms that did not relinquish their hold even when her eyes rose defiantly to his. Startled by the heat of his gaze, she was unable to refute his argument. Then, collecting her wits, she placed a step between them and said in a less steady voice than she intended, "Might as well hope to teach a pig to play the flute, My Lord."

Turning, she saw the baggage coach in the yard and seized her opportunity for escape. "Pray, excuse me, Cousin. Trent requires direction."

That her abigail needed no supervision, Sarah discovered upon entering her bedchamber. The competent woman had unpacked such articles as Sarah might need for her unexpected sojourn, and was directing a porter to return the trunk to the coach which was to continue on its slow way to London.

"We are to travel on to London tomorrow by post-chaise," Sarah informed her after the unwieldy burden was carried away. Then, sitting on the foot of the bed, she added, "I depend upon you to accompany me."

"Of course, Miss."

Trent spoke in such a firm voice that Sarah understood her abigail did not intend to let her travel alone. Such protective vehemence might ordinarily have caused her to protest her independence, but Sarah's confidence had been badly shaken by the scene with Pemberton. She accepted Trent's escort with a grateful smile and an unabashed sigh of relief which sounded more like a groan as she bent forwards to untie her carriage boots.

Trent hurried to her assistance. "Miss, I know you do not like to trouble me, but I wish you will let me undress you."

"Very well, have at these boots," Sarah allowed, leaning her elbows on the mattress. "They are pinching my toes."

While Trent was removing the offending footgear, Sarah fumed over the events of the day. As soon as her boots had been removed and her abigail had regained her feet, Sarah flung herself from the bed and began to pace the bare floor with a violence that matched her thoughts. Finally, she realised there was only one way she could avoid another confrontation with her travelling companion. "Kindly inform Lord Pemberton that I shall take my supper in my room. I—I am rather upset—by the accident."

"Yes, Miss," replied Trent, her forehead puckered with anxiety. "If you will rest yourself, I shall have a tea tray sent up." Then, shouldering the door open, she left the room.

Though the Earl knew Sarah meant to avoid him by remaining in her room on such a fine afternoon, he made no comment. But he sent up the latest issue of Ackerman's *Repository*, with which she might while away the quiet hours, and bespoke for her a tea that while not elegant in the least, would satisfy an appetite whetted by the dusty walk, their argument, and her self-imposed isolation.

His consideration went unappreciated by his companion who mistakenly bestowed her thanks upon Trent for the periodical and the currant bread, sponge cake, and strawberries that graced the tea tray. The repast satisfied her hunger, but did nothing towards settling her mind, still full to overflowing with the Earl's unexpected and unwished-for proposal. That he meant it seriously, she still could not credit. It was more in keeping with her memories of Dash for him to mock her hopes and make light of her necessity.

Sarah was feeling a great deal pulled down by suppertime. She professed to have no appetite for the half chicken, carrots and new potatoes and the raspberry jam pastry which was set before her, but eased Trent's apprehensions by putting away the larger portion of her dinner. And the glass of ratafia which accompanied her tray assured her of a rapid and dreamless slumber.

"You are a sad-looking piece this morning," Lord Pemberton said when she joined him in the coffee room the next morning.

"How kind in you to notice," Sarah replied, wincing as her jarred muscles stiffened from yesterday's accident. Inelegantly, she took her seat and enquired, "Is there more chocolate?"

He obliged her by pouring out a cup. "I am persuaded you did yourself no favour in brooding upon yesterday's events."

"You are mistaken, My Lord, in thinking me so poor-spirited as to engage in regrets," Sarah replied after taking a cautious sip of the steaming beverage. "I feel as though your curricle ran me over yesterday."

The Earl's dark brows pulled together in a concerned frown. "You are hurt! Why did you not ask me to fetch a physician?"

"A country doctor's remedies will do me no good, My Lord." Sarah flinched, thinking of the lancet.

"You look decidedly unwell," he commented, half-rising from his chair. "Perhaps we should delay our journey one more day."

"No!" She raised a hand emphatically, then added more hesitantly, "I mean, my godmother is expecting us . . . she must be worried, don't you think?"

"Probably." After an uncomfortable pause, during which he crumbled a crust in his plate while she stirred her chocolate, he suddenly asked, "Did you have cause for regret?"

Sarah lifted the spoon in mid-stir from the beverage. Until she recalled the gist of their earlier conversation, she felt as turned around as the miniature whirlpool gyrating within the bowl. "Only that we shall disappoint my godmother," she answered stiffly. "If she learns of our . . . quarrel."

The landlord breezed by their table. "You need have no fear on that head, Coz," Edward said, in a lazy tone. "I shall not regale my aunt with the details of your Adventure. That privilege is yours."

Sarah began to reply, but was interrupted by the landlord. Bowing effusively, he paused in his errand, and said, "Your post-chaise is being fitted out, My Lord. I hope you discovered everything to your satisfaction."

Edward's gaze never wavered from Sarah's as he asked,

"Do you wish for anything, Cousin, before we set out?"

Sarah, spreading butter on her toast to avoid the intensity of her companion's gaze, declined the landlord's services. As he left them in peace, she lay down her knife and said in a tired voice, "I am satisfied with my Adventure, thank you. However, it does not signify talking."

The Earl's eyebrow raised as he teased, "Would that you had felt so inclined yesterday."

"Yes," she agreed, covering her warm cheeks. "I forgot the polite reply." She clasped her fingers together and leaned her lips against them. Then, raising her eyes to his, she said earnestly. "Pray, forgive me, sir. I do understand the signal honour you have done . . . "

"Spare me," he answered, near to laughter. "My poor pride cannot endure even the most polite rejection today." Raising his cup, he added lightly, "At least yesterday you were honest."

"I hope I am always that," she replied, still with the stain of chagrin on her cheeks.

"That remains to be seen," he said, downing the rest of his coffee, "Finish your breakfast, and I'll take you to Town."

She touched a napkin to her lips and came to her feet. "I am finished."

"No need to make yourself so agreeable now," he said as the landlord bustled towards them with the welcome news that their coach was outfitted. Rising from the table, Edward indicated the door, then took her hand. "However, I shall take your compliance as a sign that Fate will look kindly upon the rest of our journey."

"Let us hope so," she said uncertainly, thrown into a dither by the gentle masculine hand that supported her outside and into the post-chaise.

Stiffly taking her place, she waited with Trent, who sat on the forwards seat, while the Earl settled their account. Then he joined them in the carriage, the step was folded, and a blast of the post-boy's horn signalled their departure.

Leaning against the worn squabs, Sarah closed her eyes as the chaise rumbled through the George's gate, and down High Street.

They maintained a sedate pace until they had crossed the bridge and passed through the village of Godmanchester. Then, after ascending the slight hill which led out of the village, the post-boy urged their horses to exert themselves.

Sarah felt every movement of the coach in muscles that were stiffened by yesterday's accident. Keeping her eyes closed against the rhythmic jostle, she felt unluckily as though her destiny rested upon the turn of a card or, as the Earl had laughingly suggested, the kindness of Fate allowing an uneventful conclusion to their journey.

But a sudden shower slowed their pace, and fatigue and discomfort persuaded her to doubts which darkened her journey beneath a cloud of mischance as an arrogant driver of a phaeton and four forced the coach from the crown of the road. With a shouted epithet, the post-boys swerved to avoid a collision.

For the second time in as many days, she was hurled into the air. Slamming against the solid frame of Lord Pemberton, she was caught in the gentle, but firm grip which was already too disconcertingly familiar.

She had landed upon his bad leg; Pemberton was momentarily bereft of speech as healed tissue complained of the abuse. When she attempted to raise herself upon her knees, a cramp gripped his thigh. "Where do you think you're going?" he cried between clenched teeth.

"I beg your pardon," she said, tumbling onto him once more. "Pray, excuse me, My Lord—Edward," she pleaded, embarrassed to have caused him pain as much as having Trent see her throw herself at a man.

"Who'd have thought you should weigh so much," he groaned, unchivalrously dumping her upon the cushion beside him and rubbing his leg. When the pain eased, he removed his handkerchief from a pocket and wiped perspiration from his face and neck.

Sarah bit back a retort. Rather unnecessarily, she said, "I landed on your injured leg." Then, "How awful!"

"Not at all," he said as he replaced his handkerchief and smiled rather bloodlessly. "I'm glad the leg was there for you to land upon."

"Yes, of course you are, but I am so sorry. . . . " Her apology drifted off into incoherence. "When . . .?"

"Oh, ages ago," he said, with a dismissing wave. "At Salamanca."

Not wishing him to know that she wasn't aware that he'd been injured on the field of battle, Sarah bit her lower lip sympathetically.

"In a hunting accident," he said in a wry voice, dispelling her vision of heroics.

"Oh." She fell silent, still chewing her lip. Not far down the road, an amused chuckle shook her shoulder. She shifted on the cushion, both to better see her companion and to distance herself from him.

"Fate seems inclined to throw us together," he laughed. "Does that not tell you something?"

Though Sarah was an intelligent woman with few romantical turnings, his query incited within her an agitated pulse which matched the furious pace the post-boys had set for their horses. Reining in her excitement, she smoothed her rumpled skirt and told herself not to act like a bread and butter miss. "I should rather think it is warning me against you," she said firmly.

His eyes of a sudden became as black and opaque as obsidian, reflecting her image in their dark depths, but revealing none of his thoughts. Nervously, knowing she had spoken before thinking, she looked away.

"Perhaps you are right," he said gently. "But I hope you will think of me as a friend."

The velvet confession raised gooseflesh on her arms, as though raising expectations. Still she dared not return her gaze to his, lest she detect yesterday's mocking light there. Crossing her arms, she smoothed her hands from elbow to shoulder, then hugged her arms to her sides. At length she felt him turn his eyes away.

She darted a hesitant look in the direction of her abigail. Trent, picking embroidery stitches from a kerchief, gave no sign she had witnessed her mistress's whispered exchange with his lordship. But Sarah knew from Trent's tight-lipped concentration that nothing had escaped her quick mind.

Turning her eyes upon the countryside outside her own window, Sarah could not help feeling blue-devilled. What was the matter with her? She knew she was not in love with Lord Pemberton. How could she be? He had been out of her life for years, and his constant hoaxes did nothing to recommend him to her. In fact, they reduced her to a state of trembling fury.

She would not be easy until the chaise delivered her to Curzon Street. But she decided she would not be a slave to her dark thoughts. She made an attempt to set her jumbled thoughts along the more practical considerations—household accounts, agricultural difficulties, classroom squabbles of Fair Meadow with which she was ordinarily engaged.

Rebelliously her mind conjured visions of dark hair which curled enticingly at the neck over a stiff starched collar. Once the attractive image had insinuated itself in her mind, it would not be expelled, but grew into an unconscious enumeration of her travelling companion's most fascinating features.

He surprised her. His hoaxes had not prepared her for chivalry. He was no Galahad, but the gallantry was not lost upon her, so long had it been since any gentleman had played the knight in her life. A wistful smile upturned the corner of her mouth. She was fooling none but herself. No one had ever played the knight in anything but her imagination.

Of course, she hadn't known he could be gallant at first. She had been overset by his smile. That smile charmed, no, infuriated her when she realised again how he had enjoyed his deceptions.

The memory made her determined to think of something else. But she could find pleasure in nothing. This time of year, London would be unbearably hot and dusty and crowded. Why had she agreed to her godmother's absurd invitation? She did not wish to disappoint her dear sponsor, but she would not suddenly recant her vociferous refusal of his lordship's mock proposal.

She placed her head against the cushion, hoping the clatter of the rattling carriage might lull her to sleep, but in spite of herself, she seemed to be conscious of nothing but the Earl's presence. He turned; she heard the sibilant scrape of his jaw against the high starched collar. A breeze filled the dusty interior of the coach with his woodsy essence. Her eyes closed, she realised she would recognise that bouquet of pine, leather—and starch—above all other scents that might cloy the air of a crowded room. Oh dear. She had no right to allow her imaginings to revolve along such lines. Desperately, she opened her eyes and tried to concentrate upon the scenery.

The vista of poorly drained wheatfields and scrubbed trees was not designed to distract her from the fascinating images which had imposed themselves upon her consciousness. Though she willed herself to focus on the lowering prospect, Sarah was lost in the memory of the way he had just looked at her—as if he knew her by heart.

Staring past the bleak and comfortless scene, Pemberton wondered, would he ever understand Sarah?

She was a constant surprise to him. He had been able to predict every move his opponents in battle had made, but he could not guess how Sarah would appear from one moment to the next, whether teacher or schoolgirl, spinster or adventuress. He chuckled beneath his breath. She was unwittingly more deceitful than she claimed he was.

In spite of what she thought, his natural inclination and worldly experience had formed him into a man who preferred his relations with others to be straightforward; for in the service he had discovered associates and adversaries who were at once reliable and undemanding. He expected dealings with females to be carried out with the same honesty and predictability.

That expectation, not that he was in love with her, had led him to offer for Miss Sarah Fairchild. Such a practical sort she seemed to be, disbelieving his performance of knight errant, he assumed they would be an equal match.

She needed a husband; he was ready to take a wife. He thought he would be a good husband, because he kept his word, did his duty, and he tried not to take himself too seriously. He had hoped she might see the advantages of joining their estates, not take offence at his offer.

That she thought less of him than he might wish had been obvious from the moment of their meeting yesterday. Sarah was determined to think the worst of him, whatever he did.

Still, regardless of her feelings towards him, he was determined to be her friend. The thought was as bleak as the landscape, for to accomplish this friendship, he realised he must play yet another masquerade.

5

LADY ANNE'S PLUMP hand hovering over a tray of sweetmeats, she exulted, "My Phoebe was quite the triumph at Lady Salisbury's dress party."

"So I heard," said Lady Pemberton, frowning over her embroidery. She desired nothing more than that the Viscountess Severn should go home and leave her with worrisome thoughts of her goddaughter. However, there was no help for it, she must at least present an appearance of concern for Anne's elder daughter. "But Phoebe must have been dreadfully wilted to have left before the Royals made their appearance. Shocking bad manners."

"They came dreadfully late, and remained only an hour," Lady Anne said in a begrudging voice that left the Countess in no doubt that she considered the foreign Royalty guilty of bad *ton*.

Rather than disabuse her visitor of her mistake, Lady Pemberton enquired, "I hope Phoebe was not suddenly taken ill?"

"She was not," Lady Anne quickly defended. "But in the press of the company, some ill-bred person trod upon my poor lamb's foot. She was absolutely crippled."

Lady Pemberton made suitably sympathetic noises, encouraging Lady Anne's litany of the injury.

"And she will hardly be recovered in time for my masquerade next week."

Lady Pemberton jabbed the needle into the linen and pulled the thread through. "If you postpone the date of your gala, I'm sure no one must fault you."

"Cry off?" exclaimed Lady Anne. "Don't be absurd, Elizabeth. Phoebe rather enjoys her newfound delicacy; it has increased a Certain Gentleman's interest admirably." Lady Severn inclined her head confidently as if daring her hostess to come up with news of comparable worth.

"And how did Chloe fare?" enquired that lady who refused to rise to the bait.

"Elizabeth, we are not discussing Chloe. You know very well she has been corresponding regularly with Major Brown."

"Yes, Lord Uxbridge's A.D.C."

"They have nearly set the date, so you see why I do not concern myself with Chloe's fate." Lady Anne added excessively, "I am rather more concerned about my niece."

"Are you, Anne?" enquired Lady Pemberton. "How is it you did not invite her to London for the celebration then?"

Lady Anne pursed her lips. "Nothing would have pleased me more than to have had Sarah as my guest, but the expense of her visit must have broken me."

Lady Pemberton was well aware of her visitor's cheeseparing ways. Her late husband had been as rich as Croesus and had left her a wealthy widow, but Anne pinched every penny as if her pockets were nearly to let. "Never fear," said Lady Pemberton, setting a French knot in place, "I have arranged for Sarah to spend the summer with me."

The news did nothing for Lady Anne's sour countenance. "How fortunate for Sarah," she muttered. "But it will come to nothing, you know. My niece has turned down every proposal she has received since she was nineteen. That," she said disparagingly, "is what comes of being an intelligent female."

"My goddaughter is intelligent. Most of those offers I myself would have turned down," Lady Pemberton replied. Then waxing serious, she confided, "I must own I am concerned that she is so late arriving."

"Nonsense," Lady Anne said. "It is more like Sarah to deny herself the pleasure of your company."

"Whatever can you mean?"

"P'rhaps she disapproves of your intentions," the Viscountess suggested in what for her was a kind tone. "Sarah has a too-serious nature."

"I shouldn't wonder at that; she has been isolated for too long," defended Lady Pemberton. "But she is not one to cry shame; never has been."

"Then where is she?"

"I don't know, and that worries me. The baggage coach arrived this morning with news that Edward had found it necessary to repair a wheel in Huntingdon." Breathing an anxious sigh, the lady confessed, "Pemberton was to have brought her here yesterday."

"Hmmn," muttered Lady Anne. "I cannot like it; two days on the road. Do you intend to force a marriage?"

"Don't talk fustian, Anne. My goddaughter travels with my son; they are nearly cousins. Nothing improper in that." It was futile to sit here, setting stitches that would have to be picked out later. Elizabeth set aside her sewing frame and paced the length of the Persian carpet. When she returned, she said, "No; goose that I am, I fear they met with an accident."

"Now you are talking fustian. I heard you praise Pemberton's skill with the ribbons to Lord Sefton just last week." Lady Severn's pale blue eyes glittered with a jealous light. "Confess, you have arranged something."

"I do not stack the deck," Lady Pemberton countered serenely. Taking her seat, she picked up her frame and, though seething inwardly, turned the conversation as neatly as she changed the colour of her embroidery floss. "Did you go to Ascot Sunday?"

"Who didn't?" Lady Severn selected a sugared plum from the tray. Biting into it, she said, "It was a rout. All the Royalty were there, on time; and General Blucher . . . such a hero." She punctuated her economium with a tremulous sigh. "Not the least height in his manner. So obliging. . . . " She paused, fluttering her lashes as though she were a coquette of eighteen instead of a matron of fifty-three.

"Yes, and I suppose you fancy the general will sweep you off your feet while he's here," Lady Pemberton teased as she set several stitches in an attempt to appear at her ease. "Content yourself with a handshake, my friend."

"So I shall, Elizabeth," said Lady Severn, daintily wiping her fingers on a napkin. "But do not think my niece will satisfy you so easily. She has turned up her nose at every gentleman who has shown the slightest inclination towards marriage."

"If the right gentleman offers his hand, our Sarah will take it. That is why I know she will make a brilliant match." Elizabeth snipped the thread and set her work aside.

"You back a reluctant goer."

"Anne!" The countess, her back ramrod straight in her chair, exclaimed, "Sarah has been a slave to duty these last six years. Is it too much to want to see her happy?"

"Yes, yes," replied Lady Severn irritably waving her fingers as if she were shooing a stinging fly. "If she'd done her duty, she'd have married and made Sir Henry happy long ago."

"Nothing would have pleased me more, Anne," said Lady Pemberton, pouring out two cups of tea. After handing the one to her guest, she regarded her own thoughtfully. "However I shall not force her to make me happy. Sarah has a mind for higher things."

"What can you mean, Elizabeth? Who would have her?"

"I can think of any number of gentlemen," the lady claimed, although only one came to mind. "But to be candid, Sarah claims no interest in marriage. She professes a mission."

"What?" Anne dropped a morsel into her lap. Retrieving it, she demanded, "Has my niece become religious?"

"Nothing so appalling, Anne. Though I don't imagine you'd think better of a school for young ladies than you do a religious vocation."

"A school? Ludicrous. She will ruin herself and lose Fair

Meadow." Anne sniffed, sounding like a miniature steam engine. "We shall see how far she pursues this forlorn hope."

The butler made his silent way to Lady Pemberton's side and whispered into her ear. Setting aside her natural emotional reserve, she came to her feet and uttered a relieved, "Thank God! Bring her to me at once, Mabb." As he bowed himself out, she said, "They've come at last. Oh, if they haven't been hurt, I shall give them a scold!"

Entering in time to hear his mother's beleaguered threat, Pemberton placed a kiss on her smooth cheek, then said, "Save your breath, Love; Sarah has already vented her opinion of my driving skill."

Lady Pemberton embraced him. "Then you did have an accident! Where is my goddaughter? Have you left her injured along the road like a wounded soldier?"

He linked her arm within the curve of his own. "That would have been too easy," he laughed. "No, she's gone to her room. Come back," he urged, tightening his hold on her arm when the lady made as if to go above-stairs. "She is fine; a little dusty and travel worn." He led her back to her guest who showed no inclination to leave. Releasing his mother, he nodded his head and said, "Servant, Lady Anne. I trust you were assuring my parent she was needlessly in a fret about her goddaughter."

Stiff-backed, Anne replied, "We have been sharing our concern for my niece. She has been too long on the road for us to be comfortable."

He pursed his lips to keep from smiling as he took a seat between the ladies. Extending his right leg, he leaned his left elbow on the carved armrest and stroked his upper lip as he considered the doubtful sincerity of Lady Anne's concern. Then, noticing a movement at the door, he rose and held out a hand. "You may be comfortable now, ma'am; your niece has arrived."

Lady Pemberton rose, and crossing the room, took both of Sarah's hands in her own. "There you are," she exclaimed, bestowing a kiss upon Sarah's cheek. Sotto voce, she said, "I was beginning to fear you had decided to cry off."

As she returned her godmother's affectionate greeting, Sarah replied, "I hope you know me better than to think I should run away from a challenge."

"Never!" insisted Lady Pemberton, drawing her goddaughter into the blue salon. "I should never call you hen-hearted." She gave Sarah's arm a squeeze as if bolstering her courage. "Come say hello to your aunt."

Halting on the edge of the Persian carpet, Sarah gasped, "Aunt Anne!" She moved forwards involuntarily as her godmother impelled her towards the circle of chairs. "I m—meant to tell you I was coming," she said, nervously fingering the lace at her neckline.

Deeply etched creases drew Lady Anne's thin lips into a familiar frown. "Word of your arrival preceded you," she said witheringly. "You were expected yesterday. Do you know what people will say?"

Seating herself next to the Earl in an armless chair that faced her aunt, Sarah said, "I feel certain you will tell me."

Anne's face turned scarlet. "You are of age, Sarah. I cannot presume to rule you. But if your father had allowed you to live with me after Rachel's death, I should have completed your education. Then you might not pay so little heed to scandal broth."

As she accepted a cup from her godmother, Sarah said, "Society must have little else with which to amuse polite company if it can think of no other person to cut to ribbons than me."

"You are sadly lacking in respect, Miss." Sarah saw that her aunt's hand was clenched wrathfully around her own cup.

Scowling at the Viscountess, Pemberton said, "May I remind you, ma'am, you are not mistress here?"

"I beg your pardon, My Lord. It was merely my concern," Sarah's aunt demurred with downturned eyes and moue of her painted lips. "I hope you will not allow Sarah to rule you, Elizabeth. Young ladies can be quite demanding in their pursuit of pleasure."

Perched on the edge of her chair, Sarah protested, "I am entirely at my godmother's disposal."

"Pish, my dear," countered that lady with a gentle wave of her hand. "I did not invite you to be my companion. You are to celebrate the Victory."

Raising her glass on its satin cord, Lady Anne quizzed her niece. "Come now, Elizabeth. We all know why she is here."

Sarah's gaze fell from her aunt's grossly magnified eye then fluttered to the Earl's smile. She felt her colour rise as he winked at her and said, "I wish you will tell me, ma'am."

Coldly Lady Anne turned her glass onto the Earl. His amused grin did not fade beneath her critical stare. "My niece has designs upon you, My Lord."

"I am honoured," he said in a deeply affected tone which made Lady Severn's face flame furiously.

"Do not tease, My Lord," Sarah said. "I hope you do not truly think I develop a *tendre* for every eligible gentleman I meet, dear Aunt. To be honest, I cannot see Edward as the hero of one of those novels from Lane's with which you fill your head."

Lady Anne bestowed a speaking look upon Sarah's godmother. "*Edward?*" she intoned significantly. "Did you hear the girl?"

"Of course," Lady Elizabeth replied. "And why not? They were children together."

"They fought like cat and dog," recalled her guest. She exhaled disapprobation and jerked a heavily ringed hand towards her niece. "Look at her." Pemberton had put Sarah to the blush. "A fine school-mistress she'd make, flirting like a young gel." After she quenched her irritation with a sip of tea, Lady Anne raised her voice to address her niece. "Far be it from me to criticise, my dear, but you ought to let Fair Meadow to worthy tenants until . . . "

Sarah drew a wary breath and resolutely faced the older

woman. "I understand your concern, Aunt, but have no fear; I shall put Fair Meadow to good use."

"Oh, yes," said Lady Anne, puckering her lips into an unbecoming bow. "Your school. Well, I indulged your whim to teach after Sir Henry died. But you can't mean to continue your charitable adventure when creditors are clamouring for payment."

"Anne," Lady Pemberton cautioned. "Pray, consider the servants. . . . "

Ignoring the warning, Lady Anne inhaled deeply. "I don't scruple to tell you, Sarah, you will not succeed, either in garnering support for your school, or in finding a gentleman willing to marry you except out of pity."

To conceal the pain she felt from the vicious thrust of her aunt's sword-like tongue, Sarah's gaze fell to her hands clasped in her lap. She did not know why her aunt had taken such a dislike to her ambition rather than supporting her hopes of remaining independent. Suddenly, a flash of insight enabled her to meet Lady Anne's haughty gaze and enquire, "Would you care to make a wager on either possibility?"

"Certainly not," Anne replied, crossing her hands on the lap of her green silk dinner dress. "But when you fail, . . ."

Edward cleared his throat, bringing Lady Anne's scold to a halt. "I wouldn't bet against Sarah's chances on either head," he said in a deceptively careless tone as he poured himself a brandy. Swirling the amber liquid in the glass, he declared. "She is quite determined."

"To ruin herself," completed Lady Anne. "And that is why I am so concerned for her. Such plain-spokenness is unbecoming in a lady. It will gain her nothing but disappointment."

Before Pemberton or her godmother could rise to her defence, Sarah interjected, "Unfortunately, I am set in my ways, Aunt. I shall doubtless be obliged to turn to you when all my hopes are dashed."

Lady Anne smiled grudgingly. "My dear child, you will always have a home at Severn Park."

Shuddering to think of the kind of home she would have at her aunt's estate, Sarah said, "I hope I will not be required to depend upon your charity, Aunt."

"If it is within my power, my dear, you shall avoid that fate," assured Lady Pemberton in a strained tone.

"Thank you, Godmama." Sarah, regarding her mother's dearest friend, saw faint lines pulling together her dark eyebrows. How she wished she might transform that worried expression into one of delight. But she had put a period to such hopes. Perhaps her aunt was right: her outspokenness was proving ruinous.

Lady Anne broke in upon her niece's brown study with a disappointing sensibility. "Yes, Elizabeth, I am well aware of your desires." And addressing her niece, she persisted in her own hopes. "I wish you will think about putting Fair Meadow out to rent until Phoebe can settle there with her husband."

Sarah felt as though the weight of the world had been thrown upon her narrow shoulders. "I do wish Phoebe happy, Aunt, but I cannot let Fair Meadow go. My school . . . "

"Might as well reach for a star, my dear," Lady Anne said loweringly. "You will either be burned or come up empty handed. In either case, you will be disappointed."

Pemberton was completely out of patience with Lady Severn's deploring want of regard for her niece's feelings. Flexing his leg muscles, he propelled himself from his chair and took the lady's arm as he asked, "When is this happy event to take place?"

Lady Anne was caught in her hasty boast as she was impelled to her feet. "Why, I must own the announcement is still premature, but we are very hopeful."

"That is good news, ma'am. You may be certain we share in your aspirations. Pray, excuse us, now. Sarah has had an exhausting day." Gallantly, but inexorably, he steered the obtrusive guest towards the door. "I wish you will say your good-byes to my mother and Sarah." Without awaiting her compliance, he compelled her below-stairs, saying as they descended, "Do not hold your breath waiting for your niece to relinquish Fair Meadow. She is not so hopeless as you make her out."

Lady Anne's ruffled bosom rose and fell like a wind-tossed wave as she said, "Do you mean to fuel Sarah's hopes?"

"Don't be confused, ma'am," he said, taking a bottle-green cloak from the footman. "I am not the heroic type."

Lady Anne would not be dissuaded. "I am never confused, My Lord. But twenty-six and no offers?" The Earl fixed her opera cloak about her shoulders, then, while she slipped gold braided knots through silken frogs, she continued. "It is high time Sarah reconciled herself to her unhappy state. Pray do not be so taken in by her poor chances that you are forced to offer for her yourself."

"I assure you there is no possibility of that," he said. When she stood quivering as though she'd dearly love to retort, he requested the footman to usher the lady to her carriage. "Good evening, Lady Anne." Then he turned on his heel and strode upstairs.

In her salon, Lady Pemberton said through clenched teeth, "I do not see how such a congenial person as your father could have had such an odious sister."

Sarah took a sip of cold tea and grimaced. "I do not like . . . "

"I know you do not like to say anything against your relation, Sarah; you are too nice," Lady Pemberton said. Then, shuddering, "I cannot help it; she sets my teeth on edge."

"Rather like a lemon tart," Sarah said without thinking.

"My heavens, yes; exactly like," agreed her godmother. When the Earl returned to the drawing room she enquired, "Was Anne taken in by your charming dismissal?"

"She had not completed dressing me down," he replied in a distracted tone. Addressing Sarah in an offhand manner, he said, "I am of the opinion that she believes we mean to tie the knot."

"And do you?" enquired Lady Pemberton, pouring out a cup of tea.

"Oh, no, My Lady!" Sarah asserted quickly, fearing Edward had given her godmother false hopes. "We do not at all suit one another."

The Earl placed himself astraddle one of his mother's gilt chairs and, leaning his forearm atop the oval shield, enquired, "What is it this time?"

"A mere trifle, dear one," Lady Pemberton replied with a negligent flutter of her braceleted wrist. "Nothing with which you need concern yourself."

"Only that my godmother undertakes to have me wed, before the summer wanes," Sarah volunteered with an attempt at a teasing smile which froze as the expression on Pemberton's face told her he thought she had refused him because of willfulness.

"But my goddaughter will stubbornly remain unattached," said the Countess. She rolled her eyes in frustration and declared, "It is no laughing matter, when a baron dangles after Phoebe."

"Certainly not for Phoebe," Pemberton agreed, his eyebrows ascending in jest. "Perhaps I ought to extend my condolences—er congratulations to the gentleman." He was pleased to recognise a spark of humour light up Sarah's tired eyes.

"That might be awkward," Lady Pemberton mused, twisting her rope of pearls into a knot. "Cawford has not yet declared himself."

"Congratulations then," he decided.

Sarah saw the look of dismay Lady Pemberton directed at her son. "My dear," she said, "I wish you will say nothing. If the Baron has not yet offered, perhaps it is because he has not thought of doing so."

Pemberton's eyebrows knit together. "That may well be," he said at last. Cawford's tastes run more to the hounds than to handclasps."

The Countess pursed her lips in annoyance. "The same

may be said of you, Edward."

"Not the same at all," he protested lightly. Sarah held her breath lest he raise his mother's hopes unnecessarily. "Poor Cawford will fall unawares into Phoebe's net. I pay court so I don't get caught."

"That is the most dangerous sort of play," Lady Pemberton asserted. "You will fall harder."

"My Lady," he laughed. "I have no intention of falling in love. Marriage ought to be a matter of convenience, entered into after rational thought, not romantical ambition."

Sarah giggled. "You see why no one will have him, Godmama."

"Yes, I do," agreed the Countess. "But it isn't too late to bring him up to scratch." She snapped open her fan and plied it ferociously. "Pemberton, you are incorrigible."

"Ah, but that is part of my charm," he teased. "Admit it Mother, you cannot long remain in high dudgeon with me."

"Sarah," said the lady, inclining her nose away from her only offspring. "Tell my son I am not speaking to him."

But Sarah was laughing and unable to relay any intelligence until the merry seizure subsided. She came to her feet in a burst of energy and linking arms with her godmother said, "It's no use, Godmama. Edward is well aware of his faults." Still giggling, she added, "Not the least of which is the tendency to exaggerate his appeal."

Lady Pemberton was encouraged by her goddaughter's sweet bluntness. Clasping her to her ample bosom, she said, "I knew he would not fool you, my dear!"

Momentarily stifled by the ruffles edging the bodice of her godmother's pale blue dress, Sarah was unable to reply. But Edward broke into hearty baritone laughter and said, "Heaven help the fool who tries!" Then, before either lady could respond, he bowed himself out and strode down the hall.

=== 6 ===

"WHAT DID HE MEAN by that, I wonder," the Countess mused as Sarah followed him to the door.

Hands clenched within the folds of her skirt, Sarah watched the broad-shouldered back of the Earl, and was nearly overcome by the foolish desire to call him back. Why? To allow him to boast that he had fooled her? To crow about his narrow escape from the matrimonial noose? Even as the thoughts occurred to her, she knew she was reacting with a childish sensibility to mockery which only she could decipher. Nevertheless, she felt an ununcontrollable impulse to revenge herself upon him.

"Sarah?" called the Countess. "Did you take his meaning?"

She half-turned, guiltily regarding her godmother over her left shoulder. "I expect he was referring to my temper," she confessed. "He felt the sharp end of my tongue more than once along our journey."

"I do not wonder at that, my dear," consoled the older woman as she placed an arm around her goddaughter's shoulder. "You've had an exhausting week, and I have already accepted several invitations for you." Leading her upstairs, Lady Pemberton said, "How I wish you had come to me earlier. Still, I daresay, you'll be a new person, after a good night's rest."

"That's laying it on a bit thick," said Sarah, as she folded an arm around her godmother's waist. "My mirror reflects the same image every day. I make no claims as to its fairness, but it is my face and I rather like it."

Lady Pemberton was not taken by Sarah's docile speech. Something was not right between her and the Earl. If they did not fight as Lady Severn asserted, like cat and dog, they treated one another with the polite restraint of virtual strangers. As the week progressed and their association grew no easier, my lady began to suspect that they were enduring the other's presence as a courtesy to herself. However, beneath their facade of cool civility, they were as combustible as charred cotton and black powder. My lady was quite determined to supply the spark and fan the flames.

In this, however, she was continually thwarted. She insisted her goddaughter breakfast every morning in the dining room which overlooked the shaded garden and opened onto the front hallway, but Pemberton had already left the house for his ride or his morning bout at Jackson's Rooms on Bond Street. By the time he returned, Sarah was out, making calls, or shopping at Redmayne's or Harding & Howell's department store, or Hatchett the bookseller's. And when she returned in the mid-afternoon, laden with packages and full of news, he had proceeded to White's. It began to look to my lady as though the two young people might spend the entire summer in the same house without once crossing paths.

When, the day before Lady Severn's masked ball, the Countess had still failed to effect a rapprochement between her son and goddaughter, she was compelled to adopt drastic measures. The next morning, she was awaiting the Earl in her salon at the head of the stairs. "I wish you will go with us to Lady Blake's at home," she said as soon as she caught sight of him preparing to descend the staircase prior to his customary ride.

The Earl checked his purposeful stride and came into the rose-coloured room which became the Countess's silver colouring so well. "I know you do, ma'am," he said, kissing her forehead. "But I have another commitment."

Turning a charmingly beseeching countenance towards

him, she told him, "I know all about your engagements at Jackson's and White's."

"All?" he responded dubiously.

Ignoring his impertinent query, she continued, "Can you not find time in your busy schedule to introduce my goddaughter to your friends?"

Pemberton stared at the highly polished toe of his hessians, then replied, "When can I have had that privilege? I have scarce seen Sarah all week. You have taken her to seven at homes, three soirées, two concerts, one at Vauxhall; and one dinner party in the time she has been your guest." As he recited the engagements, he counted them upon his fingers. "Hasn't she yet made the acquaintance of anyone you consider eligible?"

Elizabeth sighed regretfully. "My friend's younger relatives do not suit Sarah."

"That comes as no surprise," Pemberton said, slapping his riding gloves against his knee absently. "Sarah has very decided notions as to whom she will marry."

"Yes," agreed Lady Pemberton. "She is most particular. And we are running out of time."

"We?" A dark eyebrow arched with amusement. "Dear one, I did not set myself the task of finding your goddaughter a husband. If she is wishful of entering marriage, I have every confidence she will find a willing partner without your interference."

"She will do it to please me," Lady Pemberton said guiltily. Pemberton choked back amusement, as she added fiercely, "I could not stand that Anne was parading her ginger-pated daughter like a hothouse rose before the *beau monde*, while my dear Sarah wilted in the country." Placing her hand upon Pemberton's sleeve, she pleaded, "Can you not help her?"

Knowing he must not look at his mother if he wanted to remain immune to her pleas, he pulled a flower from the vase at his elbow, and enquired suspiciously, "How do you mean?"

Elizabeth shook her head vehemently. "How can you be so thick-headed? You have friends. You know the sort that she will like."

He tore the petals from the thorny stem and scattered them in a pink and white Sevres dish. Smiling, he said, "I can guarantee your goddaughter will love none of them."

"How impertinent; it is like you, Edward, to make light of her situation." The Countess snapped open her fan and buffeted the air with it. "Can you be serious about nothing?"

Edward leaned an arm across his chair back. "Ah, My Lady, I have been at serious business these last ten years. Have I not earned the right to laugh?"

Petulantly she said, "You will say so, of course; it is of no use to make an argument."

"None whatever," he agreed, thinking the discussion must be at an end.

"Then the Lioness's at home must be the perfect diversion for you," she persisted. "You have been too long in the company of soldiers and pugilists."

"If that is so, I am hardly fit for such elegant company," he said.

"Nonsense, Edward, an unattached gentleman is always accomodated at these affairs," she argued.

"Incessantly," he said, rubbing a hand over his hair. "I still say your goddaughter needs no help from me. If you let her alone, she will find a husband to please herself."

"My dear, if she had meant to find herself a husband, she'd have one by now," Elizabeth said.

Pemberton sat back on his chair while his mother fluttered out of the room. Left in possession of her salon, he listed to himself the reasons Sarah had not married. She was stubborn, outspoken, uncompromisingly honest, and he thought it very likely she had scared off every eligible male who might have come calling after her come-out. He did not see how his mother expected him to foist Sarah onto one of his friends. That must surely kill the hardiest friendship. Neither did he mean to stand dispassionately aside while some poor fool fell into her snare. No, he must lend support to the unsuspecting legions who were meant to fall victim to her honest tongue and teasing smile. He must bind up the wounds he knew she must inevitably inflict.

"Why do you feel obliged to drag me to every one of your engagements?" Sarah enquired. Raising the shoulders of her new mint green gown in a graceful shrug, she added, "I don't mind missing one affair."

"You cannot mean it, my dear," chided Lady Pemberton as she drew on a supple glove of a luscious melon color that matched her day dress of shimmering China silk. After donning its mate she continued, "Or have you discovered the answer to our prayers?"

Laughing, Sarah confessed, "No, on both accounts, God-mama. I have been declared in one breath to be too young to be a settled influence on impressionable girls, and in the next, that I must be unable because of my single state, to teach those same girls how to make the most advantageous match." Sighing, she tugged on white kid gloves that matched the pert Regency cap which perched atop her golden hair. "Perhaps they're right. Dressed as I am, I must present a frivolous appearance to those serious-minded enough to foster an interest in education."

"You mean dowds and parsons," clarified the Countess.

"I did not mean to be insulting," Sarah replied. "But you must own my new wardrobe does not advance my purpose."

As they left the house, Sarah thought her godmother looked a trifle too smug. "Then apply yourself to the happier prospect of winning a proposal of marriage."

She laughed as she was handed into her godmother's barouche. "You have been conspiring with Trent!"

Lady Pemberton arched a kohl-darkened eyebrow enquiringly. "Do you fear we will lead you down a thorny path?"

"No, of course not; I know you want only the best for me."

"Then trust me, dear one. Today we shall enjoy the crush at the Lioness's den."

Without much conviction, Sarah settled back against the squab for the short ride to Lady Blake's home in Pall Mall. As she expected for such a fashionable assemblage, the drive was shorter than the wait to discharge the carriages. While she was enduring the quizzing glasses raised in her direction, Sarah reflected she could have, in the number of minutes, written to two more ladies who claimed an interest in good works or visited the Registry to begin her search for reputable individuals to staff her seminary. Instead she was being crushed in the crowd as it inched forwards in the reception line, wearing a smile that looked as false as the masks for her aunt's masquerade that had been delivered earlier to her godmother's home.

She had heard the same rumours and speculation for the week past, and was out of patience with people who had no other topic to engage their tongues than to recapitulate Princess Charlotte's presentation (which had occurred three weeks ago), voice their disapproval of her Royal Father, and praise the Princess's godmother the Duchess of Oldenburgh. She wondered if they would never tire of arguments on whether or not the abhorrence which the Prince of Orange kindled within the Princess's breast might not actually be the spark of romantic love. Such gudgeons! To think a woman unable to know her own heart, because she had rejected a suitor.

"Are you going to a wake?"

Startled by the unexpected query, but not the voice, Sarah turned and exclaimed, "You! I thought you had decided these affairs were beneath your dignity."

"Usually they are," Pemberton replied, then greeted several of his acquaintances who were near enough to interpret a slow greeting as an indirect cut. "But the Lioness is reason enough to attend this affair."

Sarah's stiff smile relaxed. "I'm glad you didn't claim you had come for my sake."

His eyebrows bunched together as if he were momentarily bereft of speech, but the moment passed quickly. His smile, when it returned, acted like flint striking iron; Sarah thought she saw sparks. "I suppose I did," he admitted. "You have never met Lady Blake."

"No, I have never had that honour," she replied, still wondering how he had produced the brilliant display she had just seen.

"Then you are in for a rare treat," he teased. "The Lioness is an Original."

"She must be, to carry such a pet name," Sarah said, beginning for the first time in a week, to truly enjoy herself.

Lady Pemberton, having finished exchanging the latest gossip with an acquaintance, embraced her son and assured her goddaughter, "Not to worry, my dear; there is nothing lion-like about the Marchioness."

"Except her voice," Pemberton insisted. He leaned towards Sarah, who willingly inclined her ear, since he gave every appearance of intending to varnish the truth. "She roars, you know."

Dimples punctuated Sarah's cheeks. "I know nothing of the sort, My Lord. What a quiz you are."

"You, of all people, ought to know I never quiz," he replied, in a tone of feigned injury which told Sarah he was enjoying their exchange as much as she.

"No? You have too much in you of the boy who cried 'Wolf!' for me to credit anything you say," she countered as they entered the Lioness's den at last.

The entrance hall looked like something out of the Tales of the Arabian Nights. Gigantic columns resembling papyrus fronds rising to the vaulted ceiling three storeys above were surmounted with capitals carved to look like lotus blossoms. Unable to stem the impulse to stare at the gaudy blue and gold interior, Sarah's gaze wandered towards the ceiling which, to her surprise was done in iron and translucent glass. Sunlight filtering through the pale-blue tinted glass dappled the company below with fluctuating shadows in such a way as to fool the eye into thinking the assemblage was being conducted through an underwater passage into the Lioness's grand salon.

"Amazing, is it not?" Pemberton prompted.

Smiling, Sarah met his friendly gaze, and breathlessly said, "It is wonderful. I hardly know whether to walk or swim." Then, a serious thought knit her golden brows together. "How can I have thought my humble house might attract the interest of a buyer with such sophisticated taste?"

"Ah, but that is why the *ton* engages John Nash, to turn simple cottages into fantastic palaces," he said.

Miffed at his disparagement of her home, she said, "I shouldn't call Fair Meadow a cottage. Only it cannot compare in elegance or . . . or . . . "

"Taste?" he grinned.

"I was going to say originality," she returned.

"Hush dear," Lady Pemberton interjected as she placed a reassuring arm about her goddaughter's shoulders. "Pemberton will see to it so you are not required to sell. Won't you, dear?"

Blushingly, Sarah exonerated the Earl of any such responsibility, as they were propelled at last into the cavernous Assembly room.

Reclining on a gold-striped sopha, Lady Blake was entertaining a cluster of admirers in the center of the gold and red-silk draped chamber which was intended to look like a sultana's tent. The Marchioness, a diminutive lady, was arrayed in a gold-embroidered satin tunic and red underskirt. Her brick-coloured hair radiated like tongues of flame from beneath her gold turban. Wondering whether the lady had been inspired by Lady Hester Stanhope's excursion into the desert with the Bedouins, Sarah thought her appearance everything wonderful, but she was not envious in the least. For the lady wore her exotic garb with no pretension or affectation. It was merely her style, and must appear ludicrous on anyone else.

"Elizabeth!" she roared. "Have you brought your goddaughter?" Sarah wished the floor might open up and swallow her immediately as many of the attendees were swiveling curious heads and raising their glasses to ogle her. Even Pemberton was laughing at her. "Bring the chit to me," continued the Marchioness. "Ah, how pretty you are!"

"I shall pay my respects to our hostess later," the Earl said. Into Sarah's ear he urged, "Don't get too close; she does bite."

"Do not listen to him, dear," Lady Pemberton urged, as he strode towards a group of uniformed officers.

"Oh, I never take him seriously," Sarah replied. She heard him laugh off the officers' good-natured taunts of having given up the pleasures of camp life for the dubious benefits of titled life. "Camp life would be a luxury, Smythe, if I were the third son, and had no family obligations," he was saying to the obvious enjoyment of their companions. Then, she was led towards Lady Blake and was unable to hear what obligations were weighing so heavily on his shoulders.

The Earl did not allow himself to be too much oppressed by the responsibilities which he had shouldered in the months since his resumption of civilian life. The one concern that had prompted him to resign his Colonelcy, namely the preservation of the Pemberton line, was not a subject which he cared to discuss. However, his reluctance placed no bar in the way of his companions.

"Haven't seen much of you since you returned to England," Smythe was saying. "Now I see why. Pretty."

"Don't take it into your head to ask for an introduction," Pemberton cautioned. "She is not your type."

Smythe threw back his head and laughed in a manner that made him resemble his dun-coloured mount. "Meaning she has no money, eh?"

"Needn't be so vulgar, Smythe," the Earl protested.

"Heard Sir Henry left her a pretty inheritance. What happened?" asked another dragoon.

"Cents per cents," came the reply. Edward scowled over his shoulder. Damn Repton for his wide mouth. "Father dipped rather too deep," he was saying. "Left her with the bills."

"You know her?" Smythe enquired. Edward thought the long-shanked pup ought to be strangled.

"Pemberton had the kindness to introduce us," Repton replied, taking snuff with his usual elegant aplomb. "Shan't forget it, My Lord. Think I shall renew my acquaintance with the lady. Excuse me, gentlemen." Bowing, he moved across the room and bowed to Sarah who was seated at the Lioness's knee.

"Thought he said her pockets were to let," said Smythe. "Nothing to interest him there."

Edward was valiantly suppressing the impulse to throttle the youngest son of the Baronet Smythe of Smarden. His ire found a new target when the dragoon at his elbow leaned towards Smythe and said, "She has an estate in Northhampshire."

"That explains his sudden infatuation," Smythe muttered. "You've land in Northhampshire, My Lord?"

Leaning his shoulder against an iron palm trunk as he watched her blush at something Repton had said, Edward pulled apprehensively at his lower lip and confessed, "Sarah and I are neighbours."

"Got an eye on her yourself?"

The Earl fixed an authoritative glare upon the impertinent young man. "Are you forgetting whom you are addressing, Lieutenant?"

The gangly officer drew himself to attention. "No, sir, Colonel, sir." Then, sheepishly, "I guess I did, sir."

"Never do so again, Smythe, or I shall see to it that your advancement in the ranks is slow and arduous."

"Yes sir, begging your pardon, sir."

Edward had let the paperskull scrape long enough. But he could not resist pulling rank once more as he told the saluting fool he was dismissed. At once Smythe executed a smart about-face and marched towards the door to the delight of the Earl's companions. When he passed into the foyer, Edward excused himself and moved towards the Lioness's party.

Feeling like a child about to be made to recite, Sarah followed her godmother to the Marchioness who, after extending her ringed and braceleted hand, roared, "Why is it, my dear, you have not yet claimed a husband?" For a moment, Sarah stared at her hostess, wondering to herself why it was great ladies so often neglected their manners. But apparently the Lioness expected an answer, for she enquired in quite a friendly style, "Did you not hear me, Miss Fairchild?"

"Yes, My Lady, I heard you quite plainly," Sarah said in a quiet voice. "Only I was deciding whether or not to reply." She heard the sharp intake of breath those close enough to have overheard emitted, and the buzz which signified that her impertinent response was being relayed from person to person.

Lady Blake raised her glass and quizzed Sarah. She reproached herself with an inward, Why can I not govern my tongue? while being careful not to evince any outward hint of her chagrin.

"Ha!" the Lioness laughed, as she dropped the glass on its gold chain. "Full of pluck, this one is. I congratulate you, Elizabeth on your good fortune in a goddaughter." She patted the cushion and said, "Come sit by me, Sarah. I'm sick to death with all the prittle-prattle my guests bandy about. Not an original thought in their empty heads. You're different; saw it at a glance."

"Thank you, I think," Sarah replied, placing herself upon the sopha.

Lady Blake affected a confidential volume considerably lower than her former tone. "Pray do not be insulted. I am incorrigibly rude. And no one dares to deliver a setdown for fear I shall put a period to their social existence. Sheep!"

Sarah had no fears upon that head, but she did wonder how many sheep the Marchioness had slaughtered. "Would you?" she asked.

The Lioness tapped Sarah's hand with her ostrich plume fan. "That is my secret. Depend upon it, your standing has increased today. Elizabeth and I will make you a success."

"Please My Lady, I do not wish to seem ungrateful, but my godmother and I are working at cross-purposes; I have other aspirations."

"Not the theatre, I hope!" Lady Blake interjected.

"No, of course not," Sarah replied, smiling. "I have been warned not to speak of my school today."

"Most of the company will be grateful for your restraint," Lady Blake said, while ringing for a servant. She whispered a few words into the ear of a footman who responded with amazing alacrity to her summons, then she returned her disconcertingly green gaze onto Sarah. "However, there are a few here who are known to harbour an interest in good works—hospitals, orphanages, that sort of thing. I'm of the opinion one or two of them might find your ambition just the thing."

Sarah scarce could believe her ears, or her good fortune. "Thank you, My Lady. I will not forget your kindness."

"Piffle," Lady Blake replied gruffly. "Better you should find a gentleman to make happy." Leaning forwards, she whispered, "Hither comes one from whom I would warn you, dear." Sarah followed her hostess's nod and found herself gazing into Charles Repton's vivid blue stare as he crossed the room towards her. She could not help colouring while the Lioness was continuing her helpful monologue. "No time for particulars, but mark my words, dear, he is extremely dangerous." In a more generally audible voice she greeted him in her inimitable style. "What can possibly have brought you here, Charles?"

His grin did not diminish as he replied, "Good evening, My Lady." He bestowed a conspiratorial wink upon Sarah as he taxed the Lioness. "I daresay it was not the refreshment," he said, peering through a glass containing a diluted punch. "Must have been the company."

"Impertinent boy, give me a hug." As he complied, she scolded, "Do not strangle me." Pushing him away, she adjusted her turban which he had knocked askew. "And stop ogling Miss Fairchild; she is not for the likes of you."

"Now you have piqued my interest," he said, still smiling upon Sarah. "Introduce us."

"What? Lend my countenance to you?" Lady Blake shook her fan at him, though her scowl was fast becoming an indulgent smile. "I will not. Go away, you rascal."

Sarah saw the scowl breaking up and said with a gentle smile, "He is playing you like a violin, My Lady. Lord Pemberton has already introduced us."

"No, did he?" the Lioness enquired in a testy manner. "And did he tell you Charles Repton has encroaching ways? The Earl is a fool, and so I shall tell him."

"The Lioness thinks everyone is a fool at one time or other," Mr. Repton laughed as though confident the Marchioness would not dismiss him from the gathering.

"I have yet to discern that endearing quality in you, Charles," Lady Blake said. "You are as shrewd as a cent per cent."

He bowed as though he considered she had paid him a compliment. But Sarah understood that Lady Blake held him in aversion, and vowed she would deal carefully with him. An arch smile lifted a corner of his sensuous mouth as he said, "I cannot fault you on that account, My Lady. My interest in your quest is compounding at an almost usurious rate." Offering Sarah his hand, he enquired of the Marchioness, "Would you excuse us . . . ?"

"I will not. Miss Fairchild is serious-minded; you'll not be turning her head with flummery."

"For a change, you wrong me," he avowed, pressing a hand to his heart as though he had been wounded. "I merely wish to enquire about her school."

"You?" demanded the Lioness, her quizzing glass at the ready.

"I am hopeful of finding a sponsor," Sarah said. "But my godmother insists I must not bore the company with such eccentric aspirations."

At that moment, the Earl joined the party. "Is it true you introduced Lady Pemberton's goddaughter to this reprobate?" snapped the Lioness.

"I could scarcely do otherwise, ma'am," Edward said. "As it is impolite to carry on a conversation without making introductions all around."

"Well, redeem yourself by taking Miss Fairchild to the Reverend Mr. Godwyn," Lady Blake commanded, pointing towards an expensively but soberly dressed young man who was making an ineffective attempt to extricate himself from conversation with an elderly lady who was dressed in a gown of lavender trimmed in black. He was patting her black-gloved hands in a comforting fashion, but kept glancing around the room as if looking for someone to rescue him from his mission of mercy.

The Earl presented the appearance of one also seeking release from an odious duty. "Do not frown so," Sarah laughed. "Lady Blake has recommended I speak with Mr. Godwyn about Fair Meadow School."

"Your school," he responded in a distracted manner, as though reining in thoughts which had run away with him.

"Yes, of course," interjected the Marchioness in her typically brusque style. "Her school, you paperskull. Did you think I was suggesting you step into the parson's mousetrap?" She gave the Earl's arm a stinging tap with the ivory sticks of her fan. "Ha! Earl or not, I should be doing Miss Fairchild no favor to leg-shackle her to the likes of you!"

Though Sarah had been looking at Pemberton with a fond smile before Lady Blake's outrageous observation, afterwards, she immediately dropped her gaze to the floor, hotly conscious of the mocking laughter which swirled around them. Anything she might say would only spur gossip and place further obstacles in the way of her school. Remaining silent by biting the corner of her lip, she tilted her head to afford herself a glimpse of the Earl, hoping he had good sense enough to refrain from fueling the gossip mill.

He was bowing as though acknowledging the Marchioness's thrust to his pride, and raised himself in Sarah's esteem by handing her from the sopha without saying anything, aside from the usual banalities. As they were moving towards Mr. Godwyn, she said, "Only an uncommonly strong man can bridle his tongue."

He was eyeing her in an appreciative manner, as he responded, "Or woman." He hastened to explain his unconscious jest, but Sarah, laughing delightfully, waved him to silence.

"I know what you meant," she giggled. "And you are right. A woman who can bridle her tongue is more valuable than rubies." Relieved when he grinned, she said, "Perhaps you will eventually discover one of those rare creatures."

He leaned towards her ear and replied, "If I do, I shall probably find her a sadly dull bird."

"Do you think so?" she enquired, looking at him with brows raised in wonder. "Even after our outspoken journey into Town?" He was nodding his assurance. "What can it mean?"

"I am not at all certain," he confessed, with an insignificant shrug of his shoulders. "Ah, Mr. Godwyn, may we interrupt?"

The parson turned an expression of unbridled relief upon the interlopers. Sarah offered encouragement to Lady Bingham, whose period of mourning for her husband had been extended by the untimely demise of her firstborn son. She did not mouth the ordinary platitudes that make grievers wonder why they are not able to "get on with their lives," but enquired instead about that lady's garden. "We have interrupted the landscaping," Lady Bingham said mournfully.

"But you must continue! Wasn't it a pet of the Viscount's?" Sarah said.

"Yes, Robert was particularly fond of the ha-ha which was to border the south lawn." The grieving Countess sighed, and touched her black-bordered handkerchief to her dripping nose. "But that is where he fell and broke his neck."

A prudent comforter might commiserate with the mother's reluctance to persevere. After a moment's consideration, Sarah said, "You must do as you see fit, of course, but knowing Robert's penchant for improvements, I should hesitate to undo his work. You might think of the garden as a monument."

The Countess brightened as though such a consideration had never before occurred to her. "Yes, that is right. Miss Fairchild, you are a godsend; I have been thinking about ripping up my son's handiwork. Now I can enjoy it. Mr. Godwyn, how is it you did not think of such a comforting thing?"

At a loss for a suitable excuse, the beleaguered parson came to his feet, accepting the hand Lord Pemberton held out. "Your lady has done in two minutes what I have been attempting for the past half-hour," said the astounded cleric. "What can I possibly do for you that does not lie within her power?"

Edward choked, then regained his customary aplomb, saying, "Miss Fairchild's the lady the Marchioness has sent to you."

"About the school?" Reverend Mr. Godwyn accepted the hand Sarah offered him, and drew her away from the Countess, blurting out, "You are the lady who is proposing to open a school in the fall?"

"Yes, Reverend," Sarah replied, pleading with the Earl not to abandon her. Grinningly, he excused himself from the comforted lady, to follow the new captive. "I hope you can help; everyone else says I am too young," she confessed. "But I have been teaching neighbourhood children for two years, hoping to keep them out of factories and mines, with much success. Those who have left Dunmead and Fair Meadow have taken positions as clerks and seamstresses." She blushed as though loathe to take credit for her students's accomplishments. "I thought a school would offer girls better opportunities. . . . "

"To improve their marital chances," ventured the cleric thoughtfully. "Yes. I think the Bishop is considering funding such an institution. After your miraculous handling of Lady Bingham, I shall be happy to assist you in any way I can."

Sarah breathed a thankful sigh. "You have no idea how you have encouraged me, sir," she said fervently. Then, turning to her escort, who was regarding her with amusement, she exclaimed, "Oh, Edward, at last, I can hope!"

"Yes," he replied, laughing, in accord with her exuberance as he called for their carriage and led her towards his mother who was looking rather pulled. "And now you have fueled the *ton's* expectations. I suppose they will have us wed before the summer wanes."

"Do not tease, Dash," she said. "That would spoil our friendship."

"Yes, I am persuaded we should learn to hate one another," he said in jest.

"No, do you?" she replied in surprise. "I should never hate you, but . . . "

"Ah, but you did, when you were seven," he reminded her.

"I hope I have put away my childish feelings, Edward. But even if I should not hate you, I am persuaded you might not like having a wife who did not always reflect back your image."

"I have heard it is more convenient if she does," he said, after they had made their farewells to their hostess.

"I am certain it must be for the husband," she replied, allowing him to hand her into her godmother's barouche for the homeward drive. "However, I do not wish to hide in the shadows. I prefer to see a clear reflexion of myself."

Although she had not been a party to the complete conversation, Lady Pemberton offered an assurance, "That is possible, my dear, in spite of the conflicting images one sees in other eyes."

"I do not see how," Sarah protested. "When one does not fit the mold, others are constantly trying to remake one into their image."

"It is more convenient," Lady Pemberton said, laughing. Sarah, regarding the Earl's amused appreciation of his mother's assertion, began to giggle herself.

Though she was feeling no ill effects from the entertaining afternoon, Sarah eventually allowed her godmother to convince her that what she needed was a nap. "But I can rest while you are at Aunt Anne's ball," she protested at first.

"You will certainly not mope in your room while Anne's daughters parade about upon gentlemen's arms," said the Countess in the most severe tone she could affect. But before Sarah might enquire what she was supposed to do while the ball was in full swing, Lady Pemberton shooed her upstairs.

"Very well, ma'am," Sarah said, laughing in spite of herself. "I shall mope in my room now, but I shall not sleep."

A quiet bustle in her chamber brought her to wakefulness. As she leaned upon her elbows rubbing sleep from her eyes, she saw a parade of housemaids and dressers coming into her chamber lighting candles and laying open wardrobes. On their heels two footmen laboured under a heavy burden that looked hideously like a body swathed in a winding sheet. Shivering, Sarah thought she must be having a very unpleasant dream. When her godmother, dressed as a white swan, sailed into the room, she smiled and lay back on her pillows, relieved that her dream was not to be a nightmare.

"Wake up, my dear," said Lady Pemberton, until Sarah assured her she was fully conscious. "My carriage will be making its appearance at any moment, so I haven't time to explain." With a wave of her hand, she directed the footman to place the sheet-draped package on the chaise. After they had left the room, the Dowager Countess announced, "Whether you like it or not, you are going to the masquerade."

"It will be very odd for me to attend when my aunt is not expecting me," Sarah protested.

"Do not be difficult, my dear; she will never know you, if you leave before the unmasking," said Lady Pemberton, tugging Sarah out of bed.

She allowed herself to be brought to her feet and, as the maids set about readying her for the still-swaddled costume, said, "If you do not know it, constant interference has made me a laughing stock in Society, and made me quite ineligible as a schoolmistress."

"Well, I cannot say I am sorry for that," Lady Pemberton said. "You cannot always be hiding your light behind a book, my dear. I wish you had not been so serious, scaring away every suitor all these years. Your chances of making a marriage are really quite slim, you know."

"No doubt they have been entered in the books at White's," Sarah said without rancour.

"Do you think so?" Intrigued, my lady fanned the air about her with her large feathered fan. "All the better. It will provide you with a fascinating air."

The dressers, unwrapping the costume, raised it into the light. The air shimmered with the reflexion of thousands of diamond faceted brilliants which emblazoned the dress. "Isn't it marvelous?" crowed my lady.

"Good God!" Sarah cried, shading her eyes from the explosion of light, "It's a crystal nightmare!"

"It's a perfect disguise, my dear. All anyone will see looking at you is light and glimpses of themselves. You'll outshine your cousins and dazzle every unattached male in Anne's house. She will turn positively green."

For a moment, Sarah was convinced her godmother was a raving lunatic. How, she wondered, was anyone to know she was outshining her cousins, if she was to leave before the unmasking? And if she did not escape, she would never be esteemed in polite society again. Still, if she did not go, she would be doomed to stuffy drawing rooms and their boring tittle tattle for the rest of the summer. It would be fun to do something so completely unexpected of one, something at once dangerous and utterly harmless.

Suddenly becoming captivated by the absurdity of her godmother's plans, and breaking into laughter, Sarah hugged the lady. "I was wrong, ma'am. This is no dream; it's madness. We will both be carted to Bedlam!"

"Very possibly, my dear," concurred the Swan. "But won't it be fun?"

By the time she was handed, swathed in a voluminous black velvet cloak, into an antique gilt berlin coach, Sarah was less certain her adventure would be "fun". The silver chemise and brilliant overdress and hood were abominably heavy. And the sparking adornments that glittered most delightfully in the lamplight, now pricked like the tortures of hell.

7

AN HOUR HAD passed since the last coach had deposited its gaily caparisoned occupants at Lady Severn's door. When her own carriage drew up at the brightly lighted mansion in Hanover Square, Sarah paused a moment after her footman had lowered the step, then, taking a shaky breath to fortify herself for the crush within, released the silver clasps and dropped her cloak to the worn velvet cushions, then accepted her man's hand to descend from the coach. Alone, she climbed the front steps.

She stood on the threshold, wishing the door might remain closed to her, but open it did, shocking her aunt's normally stoical butler into an involuntary "Gad!" before he ushered the brilliant newcomer into the crowded townhouse. The crystals and brilliants which adorned the Sparkler's silver gown and hooded mask tinkled insistently, attracting all the more notice until every head was turned towards her.

The company stared, unmoving. The Sparkler seemed to be the only person capable of movement except for Phoebe. Clutching the black and white skirt of her harlequin costume in a fist, the poorly disguised red-head was flouncing furiously towards her mother. The Sparkler also directed her steps towards her aunt, who, mesmerized by the glittering apparition coming towards her, ignored her own daughter's complaints.

Radiating a smile which reflected more confidence than she felt, she reached forth her hand, which was gloved in silver lace, and said, *"Bon soir, Madam, Mademoiselle; pardonnez-moi. Je suis en retard pour votre bal masqué.* She shook her head regretfully, creating a crystalline echo, and hoped she need not explain herself.

Lady Severn, startled out of her customary hauteur by the unexpected brilliance and accent of the latecomer, stammered, "But of course, Madame . . . " She even made a curtsey.

In dread of her relative's realising who she was, Sarah raised her aunt and said, *"Mais, non, s'il vous plaît."* She was hotly conscious of a speculative buzz over the curtsey and title. Who did they take her for—Royalty? Overhearing the excitedly whispered conjectures, she discovered to her horrour that was indeed the company's collective mistake.

What had her godmother done? Glancing covertly at a smugly smiling swan, the Sparkler shot daggers at Lady Pemberton who waved her on with her fan, thoroughly enjoying the sensation she had created. There would be time later, she decided, to ask my lady how she intended her goddaughter to survive the gossip she had inspired.

At that moment, however, she had no time for regrets or recriminations. Without regard to protocol the assemblage was surging forwards demanding to be presented to her. Clinging with a silver-gloved hand to her aunt's fingers, she said hesitantly, *"Madame, Je viens. . . ."* What had she come for? *"Je viens parce que je veux danser,"* she finished lamely.

Her wish was the company's command. The musicians initiated another set, striking up a quadrille. Immediately, those gentlemen not already obliged to dance with other young ladies, descended *en masse* upon the Sparkler. She accepted not the most dashing invitation nor the most persistent, but tapped on the shoulder a shy gentleman who was wearing the court dress of a Cavalier. Her partner seemed inordinately nervous, as he kept opening his mouth as though attempting to make conversation, when he would forget the steps and lapse into jittery silence.

The reason for his uneasiness soon became apparent. She

glimpsed an angry young lady whose costume corresponded with that of the gentleman with whom Sarah was dancing, staring at them as she paced a corner of the dance floor. Realising she had inadvertently separated two lovers, the Sparkler persisted in the dance, but at the end of the set, directed the Cavalier to the corner in which the unhappy young lady had placed herself. "I thank you for allowing me to dance with your gentleman," she said with a smile. "But I can see you belong together." The young lady's countenance brightened considerably when her skittish Cavalier swept a gallant bow, giving the Sparkler the opportunity to slip away for the next set with a gentleman who was casting calf's eyes at a haughty young miss who grew more interested the longer he danced with the Sparkler.

The set concluded, the Sparkler gave her partner into the keeping of one who might otherwise have considered her a rival. At once her hand was rather forcefully taken by a Roman Centurion whose blonde hair curled incongruously beneath his helmet. "I believe this is my dance," he said fiercely, silencing the claims of other aspirants to her hand.

"Ah, Mr. Repton," the Sparkler demurred. "I tremble in fear."

"Not you," he said, saluting her with a thump of his fist against his leather breastplate. "But you ought to."

"Why?" she enquired as she placed her hand atop his and proceeded down the twin row of dancers.

"Without a doubt, the Sparkler will be the talk of the Town," he said.

"I am well aware of the excitement she has caused," Sarah said, without missing a step. "But knowing the *ton*, they will soon tire of this person you call the 'Sparkler,' and. . . . "

"You are one and the same," he said as he led her through a turn.

"I know who I am, sir, and I am as far removed from that glittering apparition as you are from the Roman Legions."

"How brave you are," he replied. "To speak as though you are in no danger from the gossips."

"I am not afraid of talk, sir."

He chuckled, but the laughter rang false to her ears.

"What do you find so amusing?" she enquired uneasily.

"You, Miss Fairchild."

Her heart skipped a beat, and she stumbled when Mr. Repton handed her off. Forcing herself to concentrate upon the steps of the dance, she managed to appear unruffled until her hand was again possessed by the Centurion.

"How . . .?"

"Quite easily," he said. "No other lady in my acquaintance would willingly surrender a partner to another lady. You have given up two gentlemen, both as rich as Croesus."

"What has that got to do with me?"

He tutted, shattering what little composure she had left. "Come now," She said in desperation, "Everyone knows Miss Sarah Fairchild depends upon marrying a wealthy gentleman."

Her attempt to dissuade him failed. "Cheer up," he said with a squeeze of her hand. "Your predicament is not so unusual. I have been thinking since Lady Blake's at home I might even be persuaded to help you out."

Her mouth felt as if it was stuffed with cotton batting. Running a dry tongue over parched lips, she said, "I don't need your help."

"You need my help more than you know. So far, I am the only person to divine your true identity."

"I hope you will not be so cruel . . . "

"I do not intend to bandy your name about needlessly, but my silence does have a price." He spoke warmly, but her blood ran cold. "Shall we discuss terms tomorrow afternoon?"

If he had been anyone but a friend of the Earl's, she would have left the floor. Still, she did not intend to be spoken to in such a manner. "I do not think I can . . . "

"I do not think you can refuse," he said as the music came to a close and he returned her to their hostess.

94

The Earl of Pemberton felt strangely drawn to this Sparkler. But seeing innumerable other gentlemen, including Repton, making cakes of themselves over her, he remained aloof through two more sets. As the Sparkler gave a dance to yet another costumed buffoon, he appointed himself the protector of that gentleman's lady who just happened to be Miss Phoebe Severn. "I am certain that the Sparkler means to return your beau when she has finished this set," he said.

"I'm not certain I want him returned," Phoebe replied, pouting.

"Perhaps we might effect an exchange," he suggested. "Your partner for hers?"

Phoebe's smile rivalled the brilliance of the Sparkler's costume. "Oh yes, that will do!" she said as she accepted Lord Pemberton's strong arm. "Oh, dear," she crumpled as the musicians began to play a waltz. "Mama doesn't like me to waltz!"

"I can hardly set you down now," Edward said drily, "Without Lord Cawford calling me out." He led them through a turn. Phoebe gasped. "Will you at least look as if you are enjoying this tortuous dance?"

"Oh!" she squeaked. "Yes, of course." She smiled weakly. "Is this better?"

Lord Pemberton grinned. "I think you will soon be much happier." He led her through another turn, smiling although the pressure on his leg irritated the old injury. Finally, they reached the other couple.

"Philip!" exclaimed Phoebe as they collided. Turning guiltily, the gentleman dropped his hold on the Sparkler and caught the young lady before she was crushed in the onslaught of the dance.

In the same moment, Lord Pemberton took up Cawford's abandoned lady and whirled her away from the reunited couple. "I think you have brokered your last match this evening," he said close to her ear, or rather where he fancied her ear might be if she weren't encased in the dazzling disguise.

She tilted her face upwards and leaned against his muscular arm as they executed a giddy turn. "My Lord," she began, and, interrupted by an irritating cough that made her gown shake as if it might shatter into tiny pieces, was forced into silence. Finally, huskily, "You underestimate my ability. Any number of females in this room would die for your affection, Lord Pemberton."

"You know me?" he asked.

"*Mais certainment,*" she teased. "You are not incognito." He was attired in court dress—blue frock coat with gilt buttons, white breeches, stockings and black kid slippers.

"Then you have the advantage over me, for I cannot think who you are." Edward dipped and turned, grimacing as the weight of the dance fell momentarily on his bad leg.

She saw the shadow darken his handsome face and ventured uncertainly, "Perhaps you do not approve of me."

As he executed another painful rotation, his grip on her hand tightened. "On the contrary," he said, his voice unnaturally tense, "I confess, I am enjoying the mystery you present."

"Oh, la!" she laughed. "Then we are in agreement, My Lord. I too, am enjoying the mystery!"

She might well enjoy it, he thought; she was not being blinded by the reflections which were whirling giddily around the ballroom as they twirled in the dance. The curve of her lips seemed vaguely familiar, as though she were laughing. Did she find the entire company amusing, he wondered, or merely himself? He was not certain he wished to ascertain the answer to that puzzle, but as the music ended, he escorted her from the floor, determined to keep her at his side. "You have taken no refreshment, Mademoiselle. Will you have champagne?"

"I shouldn't," she said sensibly. "But I will have one glass."

When she placed her hand lightly on his large tanned one, it seemed perfectly natural for his fingers to close tenderly around the lacey glove. His pulse accelerated.

It would be perfectly natural, he thought as he took two glasses from a footman, for her to remain at his side all evening. It lacked but a half hour until midnight and the unmasking. Very soon, he would know his mysterious lady and she would quench his growing attachment to an unattainable spinster schoolmistress.

After taking the glass he offered, she placed her hand through his crooked elbow and acquiesced gracefully when he led her onto the stone terrace above Lady Anne's parterre garden. It was cooler in the moonlight and quieter, he noticed as he guided her to a bench at the far end of the terrace.

Edward seated himself beside her, and, leaning on his arm, which he placed behind her, gently enquired, "Have you not had enough of that instrument of torture?"

"No, My Lord," the Sparkler replied as she sipped her champagne. "Are any of us at ease this evening? I daresay not, and I am but a reflexion of the company."

"I don't know who has set you such an unappetizing challenge," he said relieving her of her half-empty glass. "Surely it cannot be your taste." Placing his hand gently upon the back of the Sparkler's hood, he drew her closer, saying, "I have been watching your lips all evening. They are driving me mad."

He gave her no opportunity to protest, but gently touched his mouth to her unresisting lips. At first she seemed frightened by his forwardness; her heart beat against the whalebone stays of her costume like the wings of an imprisoned bird. Then she was depending upon him for support, clinging to him as though her bones were melting. She sighed rapturously as he drew her across his lap so he might kiss her more thoroughly.

A crystal snapped under the weight of their embrace. The shard penetrated the sleeve of his dress coat, drawing blood. He drew back instinctively as the pinprick pierced his consciousness. "Please don't stop," she murmured. "I quite liked it."

"As did I, Mademoiselle," he said honestly. His breath

tickling the corners of her lips made her smile. "However, I do not make a habit of kissing ladies with whom I am unacquainted. Besides, kissing you right now, is rather like making love to a broken mirror." Rubbing the cut on his arm, he set her upright upon the bench. "After the unmasking, I hope to have the honour of continuing our intimacy in a more private location."

She stumbled to her feet. "My L-Lord, I am not able to oblige you. Forgive my forwardness; I am not myself tonight."

Amused by her reluctant excuses, he stood up and linked his fingers with hers as he asked gently, "Would you mind telling me who you in fact are?"

"No, My Lord; I mean, I cannot." She fixed her gaze upon their joined hands.

"Are you afraid of me?"

She shook her head no. But still she would not meet his gaze. He longed to know the woman beneath the brilliant, but prickly costume. He wanted to breathe in her essence—so unlike other ladies who were over-cologned—to hold her unencumbered by needle-sharp thorns. She was like a rose waiting to be plucked from a crystalline dewfall.

Then, crossing her arms as she shivered, she said, "I am cold, My Lord. Let us go inside."

The Earl regarded the mask which, in the half-light of the moon, now appeared to have been carved from ice. He brushed his lips across hers in a teasing kiss. "I shall soon melt your heart, Mademoiselle."

In a choked voice she said, "Would that were possible," and fled across the stone flags.

He arrested her flight before she escaped into the crowded room. When she cried out fearfully, he countered gently, "You have set me a challenge I cannot refuse. I must have satisfaction."

She tried to evade his searching gaze, but he placed a hand on either side of her hooded mask. "What would you have me do?" she asked.

"Will you stake your heart on a turn of the cards?"

"What forfeit?" she asked, still without looking at him.

"I shall take nothing you cannot give," he assured her, caressing her back through the beaded dress. When she leaned against him, as though aching for more, he led her through the crowd, towards the card table in Lady Anne's salon. In the hall where there were fewer ears, he leaned closer and promised, "If I win, you allow me the pleasure of unmasking you and you consent to ride in the park with me tomorrow." He set her down at an empty table, and picked up a deck of cards. "What will you have, should the cards favour you?"

The Sparkler tilted her head and afforded him a tantalizing view of upturned lips. "That I shall retain my mystery, and take my leave as I arrived."

The area around their table was fast becoming crowded with onlookers, who, bored with the masquerade or with their own games, were making wagers as to the outcome of this bet, who was veiled behind the dazzling mask, even as to the nature of the forfeit. The Earl had no wish to embarrasss her, but he was convinced this was his only chance of winning her.

He watched her while he shuffled the deck. She was searching the crowd, for whom he did not know. He told himself it must do him no good to follow her gaze and discover the gentleman to whom she was making an appeal. Finally, nervously, she turned her gaze upon him.

Confident of victory, he smiled at her. As she smiled in a less than self-assured manner, he decided he would try to make the loss as easy as possible for her.

At last, he lay down the deck. Smiling in the face of her hesitation, he gestured to the silent deck. Then, laying his hands palm down on the needlework cover, he said, "*Coupez.*"

The Sparkler dropped her gaze from his to the fateful stack. Then, reaching out a hand, she drew forth a single card from the top of the deck. What was she doing, he wondered, what did she mean staking her reputation on one card? The onlookers gasped, "What is it? What?"

The impatient queries seemed to go over her head as she set the card face down on the table. "The game is in your hands," she said, inclining her head and making the head-dress tinkle.

With a practiced hand, he cut the deck by a third and displayed the bottom card. "A knave," he said in an amused tone to the appreciative clatter of their audience. Laughter tittered and rumbled around the table and its two occupants.

She caught the corner of her lower lip between her teeth, as though she realised the odds of beating his draw were almost impossible. "Very lucky," she acknowledged lightly. She slipped a thumb between her card and the tablecloth, but said, "I am almost afraid to reveal my choice."

"Nevertheless," he prompted, laying his cards beside hers on the table. "Unless you wish to concede, I think you must."

Thumb and forefinger cradled her card for what seemed like an eternity, but was in truth only seconds before she flipped her lonely card face up.

The crowd roared.

8

"YOUR LADY BEATS my knave," Edward said incredulously, his eyes narrowing in frustration as he snapped his own card in half and tossed the pieces onto the needlepoint cloth.

Sarah looked at the card resting beside her fingers. She began to breathe again. Relief that she had won the challenge made her feel almost as giddy as when she had waltzed in Edward's arms. She could go home with no one the wiser. No one except Charles Repton, she remembered with a start, who was standing behind her opponent, mouthing the words "Until the afternoon." His silent promise frightened her; her palms turned icy, while her body felt as though it were being crushed beneath a pile of heated bricks. Tearing her gaze from Mr. Repton's mocking blue eyes, she said urgently, "I must go home now, My Lord."

The buzz of protest which greeted her plea rose to a fevered pitch as clocks began to strike the midnight hour. Celebrants were calling for the unmasking. Edward came to his feet and raised Sarah from her chair. "I always honour my debts, Mademoiselle," he said. "You must go."

"Thank you," Sarah breathed, exhausted by the effort to move in the heavy costume. She held onto the ribbon-back side chair, fearing she would faint if she released it. When Edward offered his arm, she clung gratefully to it, hoping he would hurry her through the noisy crowd.

He picked her playing card from the table and placed it in his pocket, then obliged her by steering her through the maze of people, all of whom seemed determined to detain them until Lady Severn ordered the assembly to remove their gaudy disguises. But he parried their demands with charm and wit, saying to one particularly insistent matron, "Mademoiselle can be revealed to be no ordinary lady. She must remain for us a diamond."

Although she hoped to escape him at the door, he accompanied her outside and handed her into her carriage, on which she knew he was hoping to discover an identifying crest. The berlin was only a shabby job coach with peeling gilt paint, driven by a consumptive coachman who spat over the far side of his box, and escorted by a footman who appeared to be more at home in Tothill Fields than in Hanover Square. "You are in no danger from the mob inside, but I cannot let you travel the streets unattended."

"But I am not travelling alone, My Lord," Sarah assured him as she climbed into the carriage. "My coachman is an excellent whip, and my footman is very good with his fist."

As the footman holding open the door sported a cauliflower ear and a nose which had been broken more than a few times, even she believed her own claim. But she was safer, at least for the moment, leaving him ignorant of her name and direction than in confiding in him. Evidently he was not convinced, for he reached into his pocket and placed the playing card in her hand, then said, "Send this to me with your direction if you are ever in need."

Dazzled by reflections of lanternlight and mirror images of the Earl that danced before her hooded eyes, she stared at him, wondering if he made the same promise of aid to every lady of his acquaintance. What a fool she had been. Clutching the card, she snatched back her hand before he covered it with his fingers, and told herself the time for romance was over; she must go home. Reluctantly she rapped on the roof. Immediately, the footman slammed the door and took up his place on the coach. The jarvey set his team into motion. In the mirrored hood, she saw the Earl was following. Then the coach rounded the corner, turning onto Brook Street, and cutting off her view of him.

As she bounced inside the antique coach Sarah laboriously removed her glittering overskirt and discarded it on the seat beside her. Released from the prison of the brilliant and paste costume, she felt as weightless as a feather. Except for the playing card that sat in her lap, the entire evening might have been a dream.

For a few moments she remembered a faery tale of light and melody and enchantment. The rasp of iron wheels, the squeak of the harness, and cough of the driver brought her back to reality. She was a poor relation, living off a friend's charity, hoping to lead a useful life. A barren existence, she admitted, recalling the way Edward's arms had supported her in the waltz as though she weighed less than a trifle. Had any gentleman ever moved with such grace or treated her with such tenderness?

She had been completely aware of him—the feel and taste of him, his slow regularity of breath, his warm, masculine scent, and the stiff, controlled manner which masked physical and mental strength beneath the smooth facade of genteel detachment. He appeared not even to have been affected by their kiss, except for the way he had held her hand, stroking her palm with his thumb, as though he had been kissing a . . . Cyprian.

Instead of feeling shocked remorse against her wanton response to his advances, she again tasted his wine-sweet kiss, remembering each sensation with joy and pain. Joy, because at last she knew what it was to love. He had awakened feelings within her that she hadn't known existed. And now she must feel pain, because she would never again feel so treasured or so wanton. That sort of ecstasy was not the realm of proper ladies. They must content themselves with stiff, formal expressions of esteem in convenient marriages. She had turned down his offer to save herself from such an alliance. Now, she realised she had denied herself even that small comfort. All in pride's name.

Pride was a double-edged sword that had severed her from her last chance for love. She looked at the picture of the stoic lady printed upon the face of the card and considered casting aside her high notions of propriety and dignity by confessing her masquerade to him. But she could not; the most terrible consequence of the evening would be having Edward turn from her in revulsion. That she could not bear. She was still trapped within the glittering costume.

At that moment, the coachman halted his team before her godmother's home. "'Ere y'are, Miss. Home ag'in, all right an' tight." The footman snapped open the door.

Clutching the black cape desperately around her shoulders, she dashed into the house.

After Trent had erased all traces of the Sparkler, Sarah, wrapped in a paisley shawl, sat in a leather armchair before a small fire in the library grate. She regarded the card upon which she had staked her reputation. She turned the card over and over, attempting to read her future. However she read it, whether or not she kept the card or gave it back to the Earl, the years ahead loomed bleak and lonely. A tear slid down her cheek.

The front door slammed.

She started guiltily and wiped the moisture from her eyes, before shakily tucking the card between the cushion and the frame of the chair.

The sounds of footsteps preceded Lord Pemberton's entry. "How long have you been here?" he demanded, moving restlessly towards the mantle.

"Not long, My Lord," she replied, nervously spreading her blue sprigged muslin skirt over the edge of the card. Seeing that his neck-cloth was crumpled; his hair windblown, as though he had ridden home without his hat, she quipped, "I thought you went to a ball. It appears to have been a brawl. Or perhaps you've been coursing the hares."

"Hardly," he said in a distracted tone of voice. He tugged on the bellpull as he glared at his reflexion in the chimney-piece. "Although you might say I was engaged in a wild goose chase."

"For what reason?" she enquired. How she longed to ease

his anguish. He was enchanted by an ice-crystal lady who would melt if he tried to hold her in his arms. The realisation that he must prefer an illusion to her hurt her more than she wanted to own.

He was staring at her darkly as though attempting to divine her thoughts. Disconcerted by his shadowed stare, she tucked her shawl more securely around her shoulders. Still confused by the prismatic haze through which she had viewed the masquerade ball, Sarah thought she saw suspicion in his unreadable expression. She shivered.

He placed himself in the twin to her chair. "I believe she resides nearby," he said absently, then directed a sleepy footman to bring them brandy and a glass of sherry. Waiting until the servant had left, he continued. "For I caught sight of her coach turning onto Hill Street."

Sarah fingered her temples to conceal the shadow of anxiety. Had he seen the coach stop at this very door? But she compelled her hands to fold tranquilly in her lap as she enquired innocently, "Of whom do you speak?"

He tugged on his neck-cloth, disarranging it into a mockery of the *Trone d'Amour*. "I do not know." He clenched his hand several times before he placed it atop the armrest.

The footman returned with two glasses on a tray. After they had been served, Edward confessed, "A mysterious lady." Swirling the glass, he raised the glass to his lips in restless movements which were foreign to his thoughtful nature, then gave her an account of the evening.

She regarded his agitation with alarm. Had she known the disturbance she would cause by her masquerade, she would have defied her godmother's wishes and stayed home. But she had gone, she had enjoyed herself, and now she must live with the consequences of what she must now believe was folly.

Taking a sip of the sherry, she made an attempt to break the spell which enchanted her companion. "Perhaps you ought to be relieved that her acquaintance was denied you."

He ran his fingers through his black hair. "Relieved? I

shall not be at ease until that diamond owns herself."

A nervous giggle escaped her throat. She came to her feet, strolled towards the window, and peered through the honey-coloured liquid in her glass into the darkness. "I am sorry the evening left you dissatisfied." His evening had certainly been less satisfying than her own. Why had he not seen through the disguise from the beginning? Was there some way she could treat it as a joke they could share? She was keenly disappointed that he had not seen the woman beneath the glitter. In his arms tonight, she had felt safe and cherished. Now, she felt nothing but remorse.

Outside, a breeze wafted a tendril of yellow fog past the blackened window. She shivered and splattered sherry on the skirt of her gown.

At once, he came to her side. "You are tired, and I am complaining to you. Come, Sarah, sit down, before you faint." Enfolding her in one strong arm, he placed her in an armchair which was closer to the firelight, before brushing with his handkerchief at the stain that streaked the hem.

His touch ignited a fire that coursed through her veins. She endured his ministrations silently for a few moments. Finally, unable to bear his solicitation any longer, she stayed his hand. "I pray you do not trouble yourself, My Lord."

"It is no trouble," he assured her. Pocketing the cloth, he sat beside her. She gazed at him through a glimmer of tears, then lowered her lashes, for she could no longer bear to see the friendly concern with which he watched her. "I wish you had gone," he said. "Then I should not have been made such a nodcock."

Struck by the absurdity which he declared, she could not help but enquire, "Are you saying my company is preferable to that of this mysterious lady who has so taken your breath away?" When his face reddened, her lip upturned at one corner. "It is as I thought." Leaning her head against the leather earpiece, she flung her wrist over her brow in a display of injured sensibility. When Edward remarked that her performance rivalled any of Mrs. Siddons's, Sarah sensibly lowered her arm and answered, "I am glad we are friends."

"Are you?" After taking a sip from his glass he asked, "Why is that?"

She tasted her wine, remarking in an offhanded way, "Why, if I were not your friend, I must be jealous of this diamond." She raised her glass again, and was not as successful this time in appearing nonchalant. "Even so, I own I do not wish to hear more of this mythological creature."

He leaned forwards in his chair. "No myth; I assure you she was quite real."

Please, she thought, closing her eyes, do not regale me with a catalogue of the Sparkler's charms. Aloud, "I pray you will not try to convince me, My Lord. I have the Headache and would prove a sorry listener."

"Poor Sarah," he said, rising to assist her to her feet. "I shall take you upstairs. You will go to bed and sleep until noon." He supported her weight up the two flights of stairs, all the while offering encouragement as if she were a sickly and irritable child who needed inducements to recover her health. "If you are feeling up to it tomorrow, I shall drive you around Hyde Park at four. And you may have an ice at Gunter's."

Edward's cheerfulness she endured in resentful misery. Why, she fumed, must she fall in love with a man who was infatuated with a brilliant illusion? His right hand pressing upon the small of her back, where it had earlier rested during the dance and the embrace they had shared at the ball, burned an imprint which would not soon fade away. His every touch, every glance seared her as his possession, though he must care no longer to claim her. A mysterious lady had won his heart and broken hers. She stumbled on her hem.

He caught her elbows awkwardly, then drew her nearer. Edward was holding her much too close to be comfortable. Against her legs, his thigh muscles tensed as though he were preparing to carry her to heaven only knew where, and his solid chest pressing against her bosom, made it all but impossible to breathe. As he lowered his mouth to hers, Sarah was nearly overcome with desire. But her regretful pride compelled her to say, "My Lord, please. You are under a spell which has nothing to do with me."

"Do you think so?" he enquired, not at all dissuaded. "What I feel has nothing to do with spells. It is real, not make-believe."

"Then it will not disappear in the morning light," she said tearfully, managing to disentangle herself from his twining arms. Scurrying up the last of the stairs, she paused on the top step and gazed at him from over her shoulder. "Good night, my friend." Then she disappeared down the dark hallway.

Retracing his steps to the library, Edward admitted he had never so disliked the word "friend" as he did at that moment. By his own suggestion he had doomed them to that remote connexion. He sat in a chair which faced the dying firelight and poured himself another brandy, hoping the fiery liquid would clear his brain. He freely admitted that he was dazzled by a blinding vision of light, but love the Sparkler he did not. What he felt for her would cool, if only he could possess her. What he felt for Sarah, he did not exactly understand, but passion was only part of it.

Respect; how could he not respect a lady who refused to marry him on the grounds she did not love him. Raising his glass, he toasted her resolve.

Exasperation, most assuredly, when her refusal meant she must live the poorest sort of life for a gently bred female. For the sake of her pride, she would eat humble pie the rest of her life. He swallowed a burning draught of brandy, then dashed the crystal glass against the marble hearth to vent his frustration.

Admiration, for her determination to support herself. And concern because he knew how slim were her chances.

She had faced criticism, ridicule, and discouragement from the very people whom she expected to support her. Yet she went blithely on, talking about her school to any and all who might turn a sympathetic ear. Except to himself.

He cursed himself for his hasty condemnation. "I wouldn't give you a groat for your school," indeed. Even if he were to set up her academy tomorrow, she must refuse to accept his help. He leaned an elbow on the armrest and rubbed his forehead with an open hand.

While he was thus occupied, he spotted something wedged between the cushion and the armrest. He pulled out a playing card. A lady. . . . He smiled, grimly pleased to discover that his honest-as-the-day-is-long houseguest was also capable of hoaxing others. He wondered how long she could keep up the pretense. Laughing, in spite of the coil she had woven them, he tucked the card into his pocket.

=== 9 ===

THOUGH EDWARD HAD not slept well, owing to the twin frustrations of his mysterious lady and Sarah, he was up early the next morning. He thought discontentedly, that during his accustomed ride in Green Park, he might comprehend the means of endearing himself to the lady who captivated yet frustrated him. But he was unable to apply his thoughts to such a pleasant task, for it took all his concentration to control his fractious steed. Thundercloud bolted when a scrap of paper blew across his path, and then nearly unseated his master in refusing to cross a stream.

All in all, the Earl thought, it had been a singularly unsatisfactory morning, one which neither lightened his mood or inclined him for company. Without going to Pemberton House to bathe and change from his riding dress, he headed straight for White's.

As he hoped, few members were at the club at this hour of the day, and those present were deeply engaged with the morning news or were using the paper to block the light as they slept off the effects of the previous night's revelry. Settling himself into one of the deeply cushioned leather chairs in the reading room Edward was satisfied by rustling newsprint and rumbling sleepers that he would be left alone to think of what must be done.

For all his worldly experience, he had comported himself as though he had no knowledge of the fatal charm which pricked the heart full of holes. He had been blooded. The encounter must have left him pudding-brained. He had been dazzled by a blinding flash of light. But his eyes had been opened. The brilliant casing concealed that which he said she must not be for the assembled guests last night—a woman.

She had used every artifice known among Eve's daughters to entice him, but unlike most of the brighter flowers who concealed briars beneath the attractive lures of paint pots and perfumes, she had fairly bristled with cautionary thorns. Yet he had been so besotted, he gave them no heed until it had been too late.

To a woman of sense, he must give every appearance of being a fool. And though he was infatuated with a brilliant illusion, he was sensible enough to realise that he relied upon Sarah's esteem. How could she believe him sincere after the breeze he had raised last night? Frustrated by the coil he had woven, he ran his fingers through his thick, black hair.

"Hallo, My Lord," said a soft-spoken, familiar voice. George Brummell sat himself in a chair next to the younger man. "What has put you into such a bad temper?"

As he regarded the Beau, Edward opened his hand and lay it carelessly on the roll, answering lightly, "You'll say I'm dicked in the nob, if I tell you."

"With good cause," agreed the Beau as he took a pinch of snuff with his usually elegant aplomb. Replacing the exquisite wedge lob in his waistcoat pocket, he said, "You present a devilish queer appearance in those filthy pantaloons. Pray to take yourself home that I mayn't see them."

The Earl brushed a mud spatter from his trousers and earned a vivid protest from his companion, which he silenced with an uncharacteristically gruff, "Take yourself home, Mr. Brummell; I was here first."

The Beau smiled. "No need to ride the high horse with me, My Lord. I have done that art to perfection."

Pemberton allowed a grudging smile to crease his discontented visage. "Indisputably, you are the master of the high rope."

Allowing that he was, the Beau then said, "If you aren't concerned about your peculiar state of dress, then I venture to say it's a woman or money that plagues you."

"Woman," replied the Earl in full assurance that the Beau would hold his confession confidential. "Met the lady . . . recently. Maddening female."

"Sounds serious," Mr. Brummell mused. He stroked his smooth upper lip as though pondering the fate of a gentleman who had fallen under the spell of a maddening female. "Solution is really quite simple."

"I cannot see it," Pemberton grumbled. "She doesn't take me seriously."

For once, the Beau seemed somewhat taken aback. "Never tell me you declared yourself?" The Earl, over steepled fingers, sheepishly nodded. Brummell said, "Greenhead! Must govern your emotions."

"Like you," Pemberton said, beginning to see the sense of it.

"If you will." The Beau smiled wistfully, as though mulling over a painful remembrance. "Such restraint comes only through hard experience. I daresay you will live through it, as I did."

"You, Mr. Brummell? I did not think you susceptible to Woman's fatal charms."

"Neither did the lady in question," came the self-deprecating reply. "She was of the opinion I would not jump fences for her."

Edward pictured the Beau turning back from love's first hurdle to save the crease of his suit. "But George," he protested. "She was right."

"I know it," he answered without rancour. "We are still friends. I don't suppose you'd be willing to share a comforting friendship with your lady?"

"To tell the truth," Edward said with considerable fervour. "I'll have her any way she'd have me."

"Complete hum, My Lord. All this talk of 'having,' as if you could have her for nuncheon. I thought better of you, really I did." The Beau shook his head without disturbing the elegantly arranged hair. "Obviously you cannot be her friend."

"I feel as though I've been thrown against a brick wall. There is nothing I can do."

"One thing you can do," Mr. Brummell said, in a matter-of-fact voice. "Marry her."

"That is quite impossible," Pemberton said firmly. "The lady is adamant on that head."

"Doesn't love you, eh?"

"You exasperate me, George," Pemberton said, rising from the chair with the explosive force of cannon fire.

Laughing, Mr. Brummell ventured, "I know I am right, Pemberton. Make her love you."

Turning on his heel, Edward glared at the Beau. "If you think I shall force her to Gretna Green . . . "

"Really, My Lord," Mr. Brummell yawned, then rousing himself, delivered an indolent, but stinging rebuke. "I have never taken you for a blunderbuss. But I shall be forced to amend my opinion of you if you cannot divine how such a simple matter is to be accomplished." Without awaiting his lordship to enlighten, Mr. Brummell bowed and left the room.

Edward had thought the Beau, for all his affectation and wit, a man of sense. But make her love you? That was, as he declared, quite impossible. She was beyond the touch of such romantic machinations.

So, he thought, retaking his seat, he must be ruthless. Applying himself to the enigma, he drummed his fingers along the edge of the armroll. They ceased their rapid tattoo of a sudden, as he realised the way to prove his sincerity.

Suffused with self-congratulation, he called for his hat, and found it awaiting him at the front door.

He was not prepared to meet Charles Repton on the street outside the office of The Morning Post, and so brushed off his old classmate's suggestion that they pop over to the Daffy Club where they might celebrate the emergence of the brightest diamond of the Summer Season. "Unless you're determined to end her brilliant career with a proposal." He forced a laugh, but Edward did not quirk a smile. "If so, I'd advise you to straighten your neck-cloth."

Rather than refusing to take the bait, Edward committed the social solecism of rearranging his linen on a public thoroughfare, resulting in the destruction of what had been an excellent Waterfall. However, he did decline his companion's invitation to drown his troubles in gin at Cribb's Parlour.

Thereupon, Repton applied himself to delivering a ceaseless stream of mind-numbing chatter, most of which Edward was thankfully, because of the volume and clatter of traffic, able to ignore. By the time they pulled up in front of Pemberton House, Repton in his phaeton, and himself astride Thundercloud, Edward was in a mind to silence his uninvited guest and loosen a few of his teeth at the same time. Civility won over hostility, however, and Edward, inviting the wretch inside, learned to his irritation that Repton's arrival was already anticipated. Clenching his teeth together to quell the ill-tempered complaint that someone ought to have the courtesy to tell him who was expected in his own house, he slapped his riding crop against his hessians to vent his wrath, and invited Repton into the book room.

Sarah did not hurry from her self-imposed task of arranging flowers in the library, where Maab had told her Mr. Repton was waiting, nor did she change from the blush-coloured jaconet morning dress trimmed with an appliqued border of roses she was wearing. When she let herself silently into the book room, she nearly burst into laughter at the sight which presented itself. Edward and Mr. Repton were facing one another like two dogs circling a bone. At least Edward presented the appearance of a belligerent—he was resentfully slapping the side of his boot with a crop.

When Mr. Repton caught sight of her, his eyebrows arched upwards as though he were reminding her of a joke to which the Earl was not a party. His effrontery was nearly enough to extinguish the laughter which lighted her eyes. However, she pasted a smile over the shadow of vexation that momentarily darkened her features and held forth her hand. "Mr. Repton."

"How charming you look," he exclaimed as he bent over her warm hand. "Like a country maid, kissed by the sun."

She snatched her fingers out of his hand and, made a fist which she hid behind her skirt, saying, "That is flummery, sir."

"I shall not own it so," he chuckled. "Even if the gold dust sprinkled across the bridge of your nose is not currently in vogue."

Embarrassed, she rubbed a finger along the fine edge of her nose and said by way of explanation, "I have been cutting flowers for my godmother."

"We cannot have you doing the gardener's work," Mr. Repton said reproachfully, then drawled over his shoulder, "Pemberton, I charge you to forbid her to tend to such mundane matters."

Ceasing the sulky abuse of his boot, Edward at last cracked a smile. "Sorry Rep; Sarah does what she will."

"Nonsense; this is London," Charles reminded them, as though that argument must end all discussion. "She cannot have dirt under her fingernails, after all."

"A little, clean dirt never did anyone harm," Sarah said, holding her spotless hands palm up before her. "As you would learn if you spent some time outdoors."

"Ah, splendid suggestion," said Mr. Repton, taking that opportunity of folding her arm around the crook of his elbow. "I feel certain a turn about Lady Pemberton's garden will do me a world of good."

"Er, yes," she agreed, casting a nervous glance at the Earl who was now flexing his whip and looking at Mr. Repton as though he desired nothing more than to break him in half. "The garden is quite delightful this time of day. Edward, will you join us?"

"I must own, I shall enjoy it more with you as my guide," Repton said, before Pemberton might respond, then escorted her to the doors opening into the garden. Before they passed onto the terrace, he enquired, "Pemberton?"

Looking hopefully at the Earl, she felt the sting of remorse when he lowered his gaze, as though he had given up any claim he might formerly have made. Instead he said, "I think not; the sun is rather too warm at this time of day."

"Then we shall keep to the shadows," Repton replied. When they passed onto the sun-dappled terrace, he leaned his head closer to her ear and said, "I nearly despaired of having a private moment with you," as he propelled her down the brick path.

The soles of Sarah's rose kid slippers barely touched the walk as she was steered through a miniature maze. When they came to a bridge which spanned an artificial stream that bordered a miniature wilderness, she dug in her heels and said firmly, "This is private enough, sir, for whatever you have to say."

"Make yourself comfortable," he said, indicating a wrought iron bench in the shade of an elm. Though she intended to refuse his invitation, she discovered she had very little choice in the matter as she was literally dumped onto the hard seat. Then he thumped down beside her and said, "You are quite an amazing female, you know. After our charming discussion at Lady Blake's, I was prepared to be unretrievably bored at last night's masquerade. But from the moment you—er the Sparkler made her appearance, I was continually entertained."

"That is a matter of no small importance, and not at all what I expected," Sarah said, rising from the metal bench.

He stayed her with a hand on her sleeve. When she returned to her seat, he said, "I was completely satisfied in your performance."

He grinned broadly, revealing even, white teeth which were in her opinion too long to be handsome. "Mr. Repton, I am persuaded you did not demand this interview merely to mouth insincere compliments."

"You have every reason to say so. But I wish you will not look at me with such suspicion."

"That is asking too much," she said. "After your performance last night, you would be far better received to tell me what is your price for silence."

He lowered his gaze, casting his face into shadow. Steepling his fingers, he tapped them together thoughtfully. Then he returned his gaze to her. "It is a lovely summer day. Can you not pretend to enjoy my company?"

She was not deceived by his artless pose. "I fail to see what purpose that will serve," she said, drawing her skirt away from his knee. She clutched the edge of the metal seat and glared at him out of the corner of her eye. "I don't like to be bullied."

His flush deepened as he fingercombed his exquisitely tousled hair in a gesture that was too well-practiced in her estimation to be genuine. She was unprepared for contrition. "I'm sorry," he said. "You have no doubt heard of my appalling reputation. The result of a misspent youth." He chuckled, then said, "Bad company, you know, does not make for good morals. But my injury, and other recent calamaties, have shown me the folly of my life."

"In light of the bruises you just left on my arm, I find your transformation hard to believe," she said implacably.

"I knew you would," he replied. He leaned his elbows upon his knees, and clasped his fingers between them. After a moment of silence, during which he seemed to be struggling with some great weight, he said, "I cannot change my ways overnight. Sometimes bad habits will have their way."

His penitent speech, rather than allaying her suspicion, made her even more wary. "Mr. Repton, if you sincerely want to reform, why don't you talk with a vicar? I am only a foolish woman."

"That is precisely why I come to you, because you see with a woman's heart and not with scholarly logic. Miss Fairchild, . . . " His blue eyes engulfed her skeptical grey stare, then retreated uncertainly. "I am a man bereft of family; a homeless wanderer. I have had too little association with ladies of spotless character, and too much with . . . " Again he blushed, then went haltingly on. "I am overbearing and unfeeling. I don't know how to change."

In spite of her suspicion, Sarah covered his hand with one of hers. "Realising one's shortcomings is the beginning of change, Mr. Repton."

He turned a hopeful smile onto her and asked, "Will you help me?" as he turned his hand, palm up into hers, and clasped her fingers in a desperate grip.

She winced, but let her hand remain in his. "As far as I am able, yes. . . . "

"I knew I could depend upon you," he said, relief sparkling like sunlight in his gaze. Then, as changeable as the weather, his forehead furrowed as he said, "Brute that I am, I frighten you."

"You do, a little," she confessed nervously. She turned her gaze upon the man-made brook that bubbled merrily as though it were responsible for their rapprochement.

"I cannot unsay the words I spoke last night," he said in an affecting tone. "Nor excuse them by telling you I was foxed. I was wrong; you are not in my debt; I am in yours."

The pressure on her hand increasing, Sarah realised she was being pulled into an embrace. Quickly, she came to her feet and said, "There are no debts between friends, Mr. Repton."

As he stood beside her, he clasped his hands behind him, like a reproached child. "Nevertheless, I should like to help you. Isn't it in the giving that we receive?"

Respect dawned in her eyes. "So we are told." Then, as her gaze fell, she said, "At least it can be galling to always be the object of charity."

"Just so," he said. "I wish you will let me help with your school."

"Oh, Mr. Repton," she said, overcome at last by belief in his reformation. Holding out both hands palm up, she said earnestly. "Thank you for your confidence, but you must know I cannot accept your money, even for such a worthy cause."

"I know," he said, releasing her gaze to stare at the toes of his impeccably polished topboots before continuing, "Not at all the thing. There must be a way . . . " He began to pace a slow circle around Sarah, tapping his chin thoughtfully. Sarah nervously stood her ground, although her gaze followed him whenever he moved before her.

"I have spoken with Reverend Mr. Godwyn," she said, "who is trying to arrange for funds through the Church."

"That must be a forlorn hope," he said. "Very likely to want too much power. You are still somewhat young for stuffy clerics to be comfortable with your maturity."

"Really, Mr. Repton," she chided. "That is hardly the sort of commentary which leaves me confident."

"You're right, of course. Beg pardon. Only considering possibilities," he mumbled. Having completed his fifth round, he stopped before her. "I shall not insult you with another offer of money. But I hope you will not take it unkindly if I send a candidate for employment."

"But I have no money!" she cried as he compelled her towards the house.

"Where is your faith?" He spoke in such earnest tones, that Sarah was persuaded to believe again. Then, suggesting they might, if she thought her cousins would care to accompany them, take in Week's Mechanical Museum on the next day, he took his leave, he said, to see to making a reality of her dream.

═ 10 ═

SARAH WAS SUFFICIENTLY taken aback when Mabb announced not an hour later the arrival of a "person wishing to speak to Miss Fairchild about Fair Meadow School," to consider it at first only another hoax of Edward's. But upon reviewing Mrs. Chitham's character, which Mabb produced on a salver, she was reassured. The widow of a former rector, Mrs. Chitham was (according to the letter) "a person of sterling qualities, who conveyed a proper blend of charity and firmness so necessary in one who aspired to a position of responsibility."

Folding the neatly inscribed recommendation from the Marquis of Ellsworth, Sarah said under her breath, "Of course she would not provide a letter stating her incompetence." Then, replacing the communication on the footman's tray, she said, "I will see her."

Mabb departed without comment and quickly ushered Mrs. Chitham into the blue salon. A woman of substantial size, she was wearing a dress of black bombazine which was relieved only by grey braid at the high neckline and tight cuffs, in one of which was tucked a white handkerchief. She did not offer her hand, but took Sarah's after the merest hesitation, which indicated either disapproval that her prospective employer was so youthful and fashionably arrayed in a striking day dress of raspberry-coloured shot silk, or her reluctance to appear too forthcoming.

"Good afternoon, ma'am," Sarah said with a welcoming

smile that matched the brilliance of her shimmering costume. "Pray to seat yourself."

Mrs. Chitham did as she was invited without introductory comment. Inferring from the lady's silence that she was not one to engage in worthless chatter, Sarah thoughtfully offered her condolences on Mr. Chitham's death.

She could not have opened the interview more wisely. Mrs. Chitham heaved a tremendous sigh before saying, "My late husband was truly a gentleman, Miss. Lord Ellsworth said as much as his obsequies not six months ago."

"It is to be hoped you are not too soon seeking a position," Sarah ventured when Mrs. Chitham touched her serviceable handkerchief to her nose and watering eyes.

"No, Miss Fairchild," she replied staunchly. "Lord Ellsworth himself assured me I must not turn myself out of my home—the vicarage—before I was ready, but the living will soon be bestowed on another and I will make my own way in the world, and not rely too long on any man's charity."

"You are very brave."

"Not at all, Miss Fairchild. Just facing facts. As we all must do, sooner or late."

Because she understood that Mrs. Chitham must think her acceptance of life's exigencies unexceptional, Sarah turned the interview towards the school and discovered to her surprise and pleasure that Mrs. Chitham was, as the Marquis recommended, a person of sterling qualities. She listened well, possessed a wealth of understanding of schoolroom girls, whose missish excesses she thought might be best countervailed through intellectual stimulation rather than the mindless activities which so often occupied them.

Sarah was scarcely able to credit Charles Repton with discovering such a perfect candidate for a schoolmistress, let alone having produced a Mrs. Chitham in no more than an hour. But her faith suffered a setback when she remembered that she was bereft of funds with which to pay Mrs. Chitham. Blushing, she explained her embarrassment. "So, you see, although I am very hopeful that we will be able to come to a mutually agreeable term of employment, I cannot, as yet, make any promises."

"That is too bad," Mrs. Chitham said, a concerned furrow creasing her brow. "I have made enquiries into another school, but Fair Meadow seems more suited to my needs."

Sarah expelled a frustrated breath, then said, "However much I wish you would, I cannot ask you to wait until we have the funds to begin. But if you are still unengaged when I do have money for wages, I shall gladly employ you."

"Well, Miss Fairchild, I cannot feed myself on promises, you know; but perhaps if we put our heads together, we will find the wherewithal to support this worthy institution." Giving Sarah's hand a reassuring squeeze when she stood to take her leave, she added with a confidential smile, "And ourselves."

She saw Mr. Repton during her afternoon drive through Hyde Park with Lord Pemberton. "Please, stop," she implored the Earl, when they were nearly parallel to Mr. Repton's phaeton. Barely before he complied, she had flung herself, without explanation, from the curricle, leaving him with a scowl on his face.

"Miss Fairchild! You look like good news," Charles said, drawing his vehicle to a halt in the midst of park traffic and giving her a hand up.

"I have good news, thanks to you," she said, squeezing his fingers between her two gloved hands in an appreciative manner.

He smiled artlessly as he drawled, "I do hate parlour games, Ma'am. You must tell me how I have made you smile, so I can repeat my good deed and win another reward."

"Oh, do not tease; I am beside myself with excitement," Sarah cried. "For the first time in more than a year, I can believe my school will open."

"I told you I should apply myself to your dream. Has my promise only just penetrated your pretty bonnet?"

"No," she replied, not in the least put out of humour by

his playful retort. "Only I thought it would take at least a day to enquire at the Registry. And they should need time to give suitable candidates my direction."

"Normally they do," he said, edging his way around the truth. Slowly, thoughtfully, he ventured, "I take it you have not had to wait to discover a suitable candidate?"

"You know I have not," she laughed. "I have found a perfect candidate—Mrs. Chitham." Then, more seriously, "If I can procure a sponsor, of course."

"Ah," he intoned, snapping the reins against his team's hindquarters to set them into motion. They began to inch forwards among the press of traffic. "The venerable Mrs. Chitham. She will not like me."

"How can she not?" Sarah enquired, disregarding the uncomfortable mental reminder that she had not at first liked him.

"I will strike your Mrs. Chitham as insufficiently serious-minded to interest myself in education. There you are, Pemberton," he said, as the Earl drew alongside the phaeton, after finally having manoeuvred around the various impediments that separated their vehicles. "Have you lost something?"

"You seem to have found the very thing," Edward replied, scowling. Turning his dark gaze onto his renegade passenger, he reminded her, "Sarah, we have an appointment."

She saw how tightly Edward's lips were stretched and was not fooled by his light tone. "Pray, do not scold, My Lord. I was sharing my good fortune with Mr. Repton."

"And giving the *ton* fuel for gossip," said Edward, reaching out his hand for her to return to his curricle. When she was seated beside him and they had taken their leave of a bemused Charles Repton, Edward gave his horses the office to start and said, "Or have you forgotten one doesn't change horses midstream?"

"I did not abandon you."

"But neither did you share your good fortune with me," he said tersely.

"Did I not? Well, I suppose I thought you shouldn't care that I had quite without trying, discovered a prime candidate for headmistress of Fair Meadow."

"I hope you insisted upon contacting that worthy's references," he said.

She remembered suddenly she had not thought to speak with Lord Ellsworth, the Registry, or the Reverend Mr. Godwyn. But she was not about to let him know that. Sniffing, as though the very question had been insulting, she replied, "I cut my wisdoms years ago. Of course, I shall make the appropriate enquiries. After all, if all goes well, I shall be entrusting Mrs. Chitham with England's future."

"That's coming it a bit too strong," he said in a light tone.

He was taking her exciting news far too seriously. She wondered whether she had hurt his feelings by not confiding in him. Well, why should she? He didn't care a groat for her school. His contempt for her ambition raised her ire. Raising her chin defiantly, she asserted, "Is not. After all, I shall be training England's wives and mothers."

As he steered the team and curricle through Hyde Park Corner, Edward choked and burst into unrestrained laughter. "Right you are," he said, risibly. "You shall teach them everything you know about love and marriage. I doubt anyone will master the course in less than . . . five minutes."

Sarah sputtered defensively until he had pulled well away from the gate. "I know considerably more than you credit me," she asserted.

"I sincerely hope not," he gurgled, controlling with a deft hand his team which was prancing nervously up Piccadilly.

She felt her ears redden and snapped, "I meant about household management." She clutched her hands together in her lap, as though she had to restrain herself from committing murder. "Odious man, everyone is looking at us."

That only made him laugh the more. "I shouldn't wonder, Sarah. They are wondering into whose conveyance you will next fly."

Choosing to ignore his dart, she took the offensive. "I suppose you know more about the art of marriage than I do?"

"I fancy I do," he allowed. "You, on the other hand, seem to possess unprecedented experience in refusing marriage."

"Must you throw that in my face?" she queried guiltily. "It isn't at all fair, you know."

"Ill met," he countered as though keeping a score in a game. "All's fair in love and war."

"I hope this is not a war," she said. "We are friends, after all."

"A state of affairs I am beginning to regret," he said between clenched teeth.

"That is too bad of you," she said, her eyes sparking fury. "Perhaps you would rather be friends with your mysterious lady."

"I think I prefer to strangle that dazzler," he replied, drawing the curricle to a halt in the shade of Berkeley Square opposite Gunter's. Tying off the reins, he skewered Sarah's gaze with his own. "If I could but lay hands upon her."

Nervously smoothing the collar of her silver grey pelisse, Sarah broke the stare and moistened her lips. "I hope you will not find her."

"Do not waste your sympathy on that heartless female," he spat out, stepping to the pavement to detain a waiter long enough to give their order.

"Oh, I care nothing for her." Sarah answered rather too quickly. "I only wish you will not hang."

"Then if I do commit murder, I shall rely upon you to speak in my defence." As he leaned against the frame of his curricle, he scuffed the toe of his boot along a paving stone.

"You know I would do whatever was in my power to save you, considering your unfailing sincerity," she said, a playful smile curling the edge of her lips. "However, I would not know what to say."

"Only speak the truth," he said, sweeping his gaze from the pavement to her face.

Immediately she lowered her lashes and diverted her gaze, to see the welcome sight of their waiter hurrying across the crowded square with their refreshments. "Look, My Lord, our ices!" When the harried servant had delivered the order, she devoured her raspberry ice without seeming to take a breath.

Edward approached his dessert with greater control, which resulted in the ice becoming raspberry soup. "Very refreshing," he said.

"I haven't tasted anything so delicious in years," she agreed, allowing the waiter to remove the dishes. As he scurried away to serve another carriage, she said earnestly, "Thank you, Edward." Regarding him fondly, then with amusement, she drew her handkerchief out of her reticule. "You have berry juice on your chin."

Like a small boy, he attempted to reach the stain with his tongue, then laughing, "Where is it?" he enquired, leaning forwards as she proffered the dainty muslin square.

"There, My Lord," she said, indicating with the tip of the handkerchief the errant drop which threatened his snowy starcher. Raising her eyes, wondering why he did not take the cloth from her, she gazed enquiringly into his warm stare. At the same time his hand touched hers. Sparks flew, but he did not draw away from the shock. Instead, he guided her hand with gentle pressure.

Sarah recoiled first, stunned by the electric current which had jolted her. Feeling as though she had been burned, she rubbed her hand, and wondered if he had suffered the shock as well.

But he only chafed his lower lip, and returned to his seat in the curricle. When he had taken the reins in hand, he enquired, "Did you get it all?"

"Yes," she stammered, balling the handkerchief in tingling fingers. "No damage done." As he directed his team towards Curzon Street, she asked, "May we come back tomorrow?"

Glancing playfully at her, he raised his eyebrows and said, "It would be my pleasure."

When they arrived at Pemberton House, Sarah learned that Reverend Mr. Godwyn had been waiting this past half hour in the library. Though her immediate wish was to hurry into his presence to receive his good news, she put off her bonnet, gloves, and pelisse, and smoothed the tendrils of hair which had been loosened from their pins by the freshening breeze which had turned her cheeks so pink.

After thanking the Earl for the drive and refreshment, she entered the book room. "I am so glad you have come today, sir," she said brightly, indicating that he should resume his place on the leather settee. Seating herself, she continued. "You see, I have discovered an excellent candidate for headmistress of Fair Meadow School. Mrs. Chitham, recently removed from Cheshire."

"I know her," replied the parson. "You cannot do better than engage her."

"But I could not promise her employment until I had spoken with you; after all, I'm sure you must be concerned that the staff reflects a loving but firm influence upon the girls who will soon be enrolled there."

"Yes, well," he began, then dropped his earnest gaze to the carpet. Rubbing his hands together, he seemed to be uncommonly ill at ease for one whose errand must be so hopeful. "Miss Fairchild," he said. "My training has taught me to proclaim good news at all times and to offer comfort when necessary."

To her embarrassment, she emitted a nervous giggle. "To be sure," she said, controlling the inappropriate outburst, though not the dread which occasioned it. "I hope you have come to proclaim. I have endured more than enough comfort to last my lifetime."

"I think none of us experiences enough comfort," he mused.

"Please, Sir. You did not come to engage me in a philosophical debate. You will find I am too anxious to be an adequate opponent in any such discussion."

"No, I did not mean to speak foolishness," he said. "I

understand how urgent your expectancy is. . . . "

"Thank you. You are among a few to appreciate the charge which I feel has been given me."

Again she was stricken with his uneasy manner. He was pulling on his rumpled stock as though what he had to tell her had stuck in his throat. "I think you ought to have studied law, sir," she said in an attempt to ease the fear which had begun to eat at her confidence.

"But I did study canon law," he protested as he ran a hand over his lower face.

"Which prepares you to deliver news of peace and good will," she prompted, calling upon that peace to shield her from what she suspected she was about to hear. "If you had trained in law, I warrant you'd have no difficulty delivering the message that is causing you such grief."

"Er, yes. Oh dear, I am not very good at this," he fumbled. "Miss Fairchild, there is no way to soften the disappointment I know you are going to feel: the Bishop has denied your funding."

He cringed in the telling and pulled from his waistcoat pocket a folded handkerchief, as though he was expecting her to burst into tears of devastation. But the peace which she had silently requested had covered her with warm reassurance, as if she were a chick sheltering from a storm under its mother's wings. She heard him uttering inane excuses and memorised phases of comfort, "So very sorry; nothing I could do; I hope you will not give up hope. . . . " But he was the one who seemed to need her reassurance.

"Please, Mr. Godwyn," she said, placing her hands on her knees. "I believe you did your utmost on behalf of my hopes for Fair Meadow School. Am I correct in assuming the Bishop considered me too young?"

He nodded and choked. Sarah went to the library table and poured the distraught cleric a finger of brandy. "Here sir," she said, placing the glass in his hand, "Fortify yourself. You cannot carry everyone's burdens; they will break you."

"So sorry," he pleaded. "Hateful duty." Downing the

portion Sarah had doled him, he choked in earnest. When the fit passed, he gasped, "Exactly his words, Miss Fairchild, 'Too young, cannot believe she could be a steady influence;' Calumny, I could scarce believe my ears. . . . "

"Pray calm yourself, sir. I quite share your . . . disappointment; but I am not completely without hope."

"Are you not?" he asked, a hopeful light glimmering in his watery eyes.

"Of course not," she assured him. "I shall have to seek elsewhere for patronage." He did not appear at all reassured. She took a deep breath, searching for some way to raise his spirits. "But we must believe what we seek we will find."

"Yes, that is true," he said, dabbing at his eyes with his handkerchief. Had it only occurred to him? She wondered why he had gone into the Church. "Miss Fairchild," he said, pumping her hand with vehemence, "You have taught me a valuable lesson. Oh, I wish the Bishop might hear you; he would eat his words."

"I would not ask him to do so," she protested, extricating her fingers from his enthusiastic grip. "Pray, excuse me, I must leave you now. I . . . shall request Mabb to bring your hat."

"Oh, by all means, I know I have overstayed my welcome," he said. "But you have done me a world of good, Miss Fairchild."

She was sorry that she was unable to say the same for him. But she mumbled a farewell and slipped through the door, immediately to return to her chamber where Trent was laying out a dinner dress of primrose sarsenet and white stockings with clocks.

"Well?" she enquired, skewering Sarah with a stare she was unable to avoid.

"Nothing," she replied, sinking upon her bed. Abandoning her confident stance, she gave into her fears. "I had such hopes. Time flies so quickly . . . "

"You are spouting nonsense, Miss," Trent scolded. "What

of the Marchioness; the one they call the Lioness. You said she took to your school like a duck to water."

"You said that," Sarah amended. "I said she was intrigued."

"Same thing. Fat lot an old Bishop'd know, anyway. Now sit here," Trent pulled the chair from the writing desk. "And write Lady Blake asking for her sponsorship. She will know the ladies who support worthy causes. And if you must, you will go to the cits themselves."

"What?" Sarah demanded, sitting on the edge of her bed.

Trent drew her across the room and sat her at the desk, saying, "They are mad for their daughters to marry nobility. You will teach the chits elegance and taste."

"I cannot . . . " Sarah said, pen poised over the standish.

"They will pay dearly," Trent said, dipping the pen in ink. "If you were to go to Howard and Gibbs . . . "

"Trent, I have no jewellery to pawn."

"That is true. But there is Fair Meadow."

"You will break me!" she exclaimed, dripping ink onto the raspberry silk of her skirt. Coming to her feet, she cried, "I have ruined my dress!"

"My fault, Miss, let me have it," Trent said soothingly as she unbuttoned the bodice. "I was too hasty. Forget the Israelites. You will find the money otherwhere." She whisked the ruined dress over her employer's head. "Now, come dress for dinner. The letters can wait until tomorrow."

But once Sarah was relieved of the dress, she returned to her desk and wrote a brisk note to the Lioness, thanking her for her kind recommendation to the Reverend Mr. Godwyn and expressing the hope that the Marchioness's interest in her school had not diminished as she was in further need of assistance. Then, eliciting her abigail's promise that the letter would be delivered at the earliest possible moment in the morning, Sarah made herself ready for the quiet dinner party for fifty which Lady Pemberton had arranged for her enjoyment.

Although the company was elegant, animated and witty, Sarah was unable to completely lay aside her concerns. But she was too well bred to allow her problems to dominate her mind, not to mention the dinner conversation, and she applied herself to the endearing task of listening to others unburden themselves. More than once, she caught the Earl gazing at her as though he were seeing her for the first time. Rather than appearing embarrassed in being caught staring, he bestowed upon her a lazy smile which she was quick to return, or he winked as if they were conspirators in a romantic plot. She began to wonder if Edward had suspicions about the mysterious lady. She had only to ask, but during the evening the opportunity never presented itself.

Finally the last guest had departed, and Lady Pemberton took herself to bed, crediting Sarah with the success of her party. Blushingly she reminded her godmother that much of the success of the gathering must be attributed to the proper mix of the guests, but her modest disclaimer fell only upon the ears of the lord of the house. "Your modesty is most becoming," he was saying, "But entirely unwarranted. Mother and I spoke to less than half the guests who bored you with their long-winded tales. You ought to go into the diplomatic service."

Genuinely pleased by his teasing manner, she smiled, teasing back. "There is a secret to conversation, sir. One must listen. Tonight was my turn."

"But why? They say the same things in the same order to the same people," he protested as they made their way upstairs.

"Never know when you may learn something useful." As they had come to a parting of the ways, where he must turn left, and she right, she proffered her hand, saying, "Goodnight."

But when she would have taken herself away, he pressed her hand to his lips and said, "Sleep well," as he turned to his chamber. Returning to her own room she clasped the hand to her cheek in wonder. How could she tell him she wished their friendship to kindle into love?

The house was dark when Sarah remembered that she had left the playing card in the library. Donning an embroidered blue satin dressing gown and slippers, she crept downstairs by candlelight. Pausing at the library door until she was satisfied it was unoccupied, she stole inside and placed the candlestick upon the table next to the chair in which she had been seated the night before. She ran a hand alongside the cushion. The playing card was not there.

Annoyed, she withdrew her hand. Perhaps the other side, she thought. After a careful search, down to removing the cushion and squeezing her fingers into the frame, she had to admit the card was gone. Her heart began pounding as though she was carrying a heavy weight up steep steps. Where could it have gotten to? Uneasily, she sat on the cushion which she had knocked to the floor.

How stupid of her to have hidden it here. Anyone might have found it, and thinking it belonged with the decks of cards on the tables, placed it with them. Hopping to her feet, she hurried to a whist table and ran a deck of cards through her fingers, hoping to find her card within the stack. It was not.

"I didn't know you played whist."

Sarah gasped in fright, and dropped the cards on the floor. Kneeling to pick them up, she confessed, "I don't, My Lord. I couldn't sleep. . . . " She turned her gaze towards the sight of him standing in the door. Dressed in a maroon satin dressing gown, buff-coloured trousers, and moroccan slippers, he looked like a Persian prince. The image quite took her breath away. As she picked up the cards, she told herself quellingly that it was the fright he'd given her that had stopped her breathing.

"You needn't do that," he reminded her, coming into the room and offering his hand. "Our servants will think you beneath yourself."

"Is that what you think?" she snapped, as she nervously recalled her own state of undress and ignored the hand that reached forth to lift her. She was hotly aware that her dressing gown had fallen open, and she clutched it closed with one hand while scooping cards together with the other. "Until recently I hadn't the luxury of worrying what others thought about me." Coming to her feet, she clasped the cards to her bosom as if they were armour which could deflect the stinging darts of gossip-mongers. "That preoccupation seems the sole concern of the Polite World."

Without regard to the grasp she had on them, cards were spilling willy-nilly onto the carpet, making her feel ridiculously like crying. Nothing was going as planned. Sinking to the floor again, she went on in a watery voice, "Compliments and condemnation, phrased in the most delicate language, intended to keep everyone in line, like ducks."

Sympathetically Edward crouched beside her and, to divert his mind from the enchanting sight of Sarah disheveled from sleep, began to pick up the cards. "Do you mean to teach your charges to tow that line?"

"No!" she cried, reaching for the untidy pile of cards in his hand. "I mean, I want them to have the courage to face life on their own terms."

"As you do." He covered her shaking hand with his own. Laying the cards aside, he feasted upon the delectable vision that was curled dejectedly beside him. She pushed sleep-mussed hair out of her eyes. It fell in a curtain of gold over her shoulder, shimmering with an inner light. "You were beautiful tonight," he said.

She did not remove her hand from his, but only regarded him thoughtfully, as though she did not quite credit his compliment.

"Sarah," he began slowly, rubbing the back of her hand with his thumb. "Is that what you truly wish?"

Clinging to his fingers, she confessed, "I can't wait for wishes to come true. I have to do something or I'll lose everything."

He tugged on a lock of her hair. "I wish you would depend upon this friend, Sarah."

Why must he always be her friend? She wanted to bury

her head against his shoulder and rely upon his strength in love, not friendship. Depressed, she exhaled a tired sigh and said, "I wish I might, My Lord."

"You are tired, Sarah. Tomorrow the world will look brighter." As he gave her hand a friendly squeeze, he assisted her from the floor; before a footman, investigating the nocturnal noises, could frown disapproval of his betters conducting themselves in an unseemly fashion.

She yawned.

"Take yourself to bed, duckling," he said, chuckling as he placed a chaste kiss on her forehead.

Shakily, she returned to her bed, with the kiss still tingling on her forehead, now confident that everything would work out right.

= 11 =

SARAH WOULD NOT have slept so soundly had she known what awaited her the next morning. Well before nine o'clock, her godmother burst into her bedchamber, waving The Morning Post. "You are a triumph!" she crowed, tossing the newspaper upon Sarah's bed. When Sarah sleepily began to scan Society news, the Countess snatched the paper away, saying, "Not that; here!" as she pointed to a bold-faced advertisement.

"To the Sparkler who Dazzled One and All,
"The Brightest Light at Severn's masked ball;
"I bid you tomorrow reveal your true face,
"While others rave over battles naval,
"We'll meet in Vauxhall's private place."

"And it's signed 'your knave'," Lady Pemberton said.

Then, clapping her hands together, as though she could scarce restrain herself from applauding the toil she'd woven, she enthused, "Edward will not rest until he can claim you," she enthused as she curled up on the bed next to her goddaughter.

"He would not print this," Sarah replied, crumpling the paper in her lap.

My lady retrieved the paper from Sarah's crushing grasp and smoothed the pages. "If he truly does not suspect you are that Sparkler, how else is he to find you?"

"He gave me the card which won our bet," Sarah answered.

Tossing the covers onto her godmother's lap, she flung herself from her bed and began pacing the floor in her bare feet. "I am to send it to him, if I wish to renew our acquaintance."

"Then do so at once!" commanded Lady Pemberton, rising to her most imperious, but far from intimidating height.

"I cannot do that," Sarah said, her confession muffled by the folds of her dressing gown as she pulled it over her night dress.

"Whyever not?"

"I lost it; hid it, actually."

Lady Pemberton heaved a martyr's sigh. "And you forgot where . . . . "

"No, I am not so pudding-brained as that," Sarah answered. Seating herself at her dressing table, she fingered the bristles of her hairbrush before continuing, "Someone stole it."

"Ah, an intrigue," breathed Lady Pemberton, pacing thoughtfully with a finger to her lips. As though she had been struck with an inspiration, she spun to face her goddaughter, her hand upraised and announced, "I suspect Edward."

Pulling the brush through her long, tousled hair, Sarah said, "You wish it would be he. However, I cannot share your optimism."

Lady Pemberton shook her silver head vehemently. "My dear, whoever else could it have been?"

"Anyone except Pemberton," Sarah said on a frustrated sigh. "He would forever throw my condemnation of his harmless hoaxes in my face should he suspect I was his mysterious lady."

Lady Pemberton removed the brush from Sarah's hand and turned her around to face her. "I think you'd best tell me about these hoaxes."

So, Sarah unburdened herself of everything that had marred her friendship with Edward from the moment of their meeting little more than a week ago. The first hoax, she began, was not really his fault, since she misunderstood that he had not come to set a price for Fair Meadow; but he did not set her straight and had given her a name she was not likely to recall as she hadn't heard the nickname Dash since she was seven. And they were very nearly cousins, having spent most of their childhoods together getting into a variety of scrapes; so telling the landlord they were related wasn't exactly a lie. But she still thought his last hoax was cruel; and it would have served him right for her to have said"Yes," when they would have spent the rest of their lives in marital misery, simply because he thought it would be convenient and she lacked the fortitude to resist a very tempting offer.

"I beg your pardon?" said Lady Pemberton. "Am I to understand my son proposed to you?"

"Yes," Sarah confessed in a watery voice. "But I didn't think I was in love with him. How could I be; we haven't dealt with one another in years; not since he went to school."

"Well, that was sensible, " Lady Pemberton said in a wry tone. "Do you think you love him now?"

"It makes no difference that I do," Sarah replied, pressing a hand to her lips in an attempt to control irrepressible sobs. "He does not want me, now he has seen the Sparkler." Infuriatingly, she lost her battle with her tears.

Lady Pemberton produced a handkerchief and said in a playfully chiding voice, "Of course he will not, child; if you show yourself with a dripping nose and puffy, red eyes."

Sarah could not stem the flow of the useless tears. They continued to fall unchecked as long as she allowed herself to fall under the cloud of hopeless speculation, though she accepted the linen square and sopped at her streaming eyes. Furious with herself, she sniffed, "Wh–what must I do?"

"You must make an attempt to appear unmoved by this contretemps," Lady Pemberton replied firmly, giving Sarah finally into the care of her capable and persistent abigail. As she passed through the open doorway, my lady added, "And tomorrow, you will go to Vauxhall to meet your 'knave.' "

"Yes, ma'am," Sarah answered docilely. Then, reverting to form, she declared, "But I will not wear that hideous article of torture you designed."

"No?" the Countess argued. Tilting her head to one side, she seemed to be considering a reply to her goddaughter's stubborn declaration, then closed the door and leaned confidentially against it. "I daresay you are right, my dear; no sense in outshining the other ladies of our party."

"Other ladies?" Sarah demanded, while Trent assisted her out of her night clothes. "To whom do you refer?"

"Well, I dare say you cannot go to Vauxhall alone. We shall invite your Aunt Anne and cousins, who will beyond a doubt command the escort of their current favourites. As desperate as she is for Phoebe's baron, Anne will likely push her daughter down the Dark Walk with him."

"And does that not worry you?"Sarah enquired, still dabbing at her pink nose. Her curiosity was by necessity unsatisfied until Trent had dressed her in a round dress composed of fine white jaconet muslin, trimmed at the hem with six rows of pink ribbon. She fumed impatiently while her abigail completed lacing the pink cord and buttons which adorned the front of the bodice and arranged the muslin pelerine over her bodice.

All the while, Lady Pemberton seemed to be considering the shape of one fingernail. Finally, as though satisfied of its perfection, she gave a little shrug and said airily, "If it did, I should not confess it to you. A *rendezvous* on that famous path would be just the thing for you."

"I fail to see how that will further my ambitions, God-mama. Already the Bishop thinks me too featherbrained to be a fit guardian for young misses. An assignation of that sort will put a period to my hopes."

"I would not be sorry for that. You are too young to be saddled with the spoilt offspring of England's better families."

"Dear ma'am, not you, too?"

"I fear so; I cannot like to think of you grown old before your time, or hagged to death by selfish schoolgirls." The Countess shook her head regretfully."What would it hurt to encourage some gentleman's hopes?"

"Do not you mean I must deny my own ambition in favour of another's?"

"My dear, our ambitions must always encourage another's hopes," Lady Elizabeth counselled. "We have a duty to our families."

"I hope I have always done my familial duty," Sarah protested, vainly attempting to suppress her flaring temper while Trent pulled her fine hair into a pink love ribbon at the nape of her neck. "But I cannot sometimes help but wonder whether my father ever considered his duty to me."

Lady Pemberton inhaled sharply. "Sarah, I am shocked!"

"I meant no disrespect, ma'am. I know Papa did not purchase his lieutenant colonelcy intending to die before repaying the debt he incurred. But I think he cannot have considered the size of his previous obligations. I did the best I could to repay them, but I have nothing now, except my house and land, and I hope, some intelligence with which to make my way in the world."

"Sir Henry did not expect you to make your way in the world, Sarah. He wanted you to marry."

Sarah exhaled a little sigh before she confessed, "I have learned to live without that expectation."

"Must you? Edward offered marriage."

"Why? Out of filial duty? Pity?" To her dismay, Sarah realised she was about to cry again. She clenched her fingernails into the flesh of her palm and proceeded, "Or for the convenience of having a wife who would be so grateful to have received an offer, she must make no demands upon him?"

"That doesn't sound like Edward," Lady Pemberton said. Then she shrugged. "There are worse reasons to make a marriage, my dear."

Sarah also shrugged. "Perhaps one day, I shall have the leisure to consider them. Today, I must think of my school."

"Well, in that case," the Countess said, waving negligently, "Mabb said several persons had called about that very thing this morning."

"Really, Godmama," Sarah chided, placing her feet into pink satin sandals and moving towards the door. "This is too bad. I have been fretting over a frippery party and a baseless proposal while I could have been attending to serious business."

"My dear, it has long been my opinion that business will take care of itself," Lady Pemberton said. "However, I must still concern myself with who will be taking care of you."

Laughing, Sarah embraced her. "I can see it is of no use to insist I am quite capable of taking care of myself."

She left while her godmother and abigail were exchanging looks which communicated their conviction in her inability to do precisely that, and made her way to the entrance hall, where Mabb was icily informing another candidate for employment with Fair Meadow that "Miss was not at home to callers."

"Thank you, Mabb," Sarah said. "You may tell the lady I shall see her in the book room."

The butler bestowed a doubtful look upon his employer's goddaughter, as though decrying her determination to be "in" to this particular individual, but when she had taken herself into the book room, he allowed the candidate to enter the house. "Follow me," he frostily intoned.

If Sarah had been expecting another Mrs. Chitham to present herself, she was sadly disappointed. But she did not allow her countenance to register the dismay she felt when Mabb led this person into the book room, even though she might have told from the gaudy purple dress and rouged cheeks that this woman was not in the least suitable for a position of trust, despite the incongruously neat muslin cap which tried to conceal a tangled mop of black curls.

"Good mornin', me ledéy,"said the person, extending a

grimy gloved hand. "Name's Maggie Turpin, at your service."

The hand thrust forwards very nearly into Sarah's face.

Sarah however, did not take Miss Turpin's hand. She stared at it until Maggie finally lowered it to her side. Without inviting her caller to sit, Sarah said, "Miss Turpin, ..."

"Maggie," came the confidential interruption.

"Miss Turpin," Sarah said, refusing to offer a more cordial welcome. "How came you to be directed to me?"

"A gentleman let slip wi'word o' yer school. Tol' mese'f I orter suit roit fine, as I know ever'thin' dur is t' know 'bout girls." She winked knowingly and said, "The things I c'd tell yer."

"I wish you will keep them to yourself," Sarah said, rising from the leather chair as an indication that the interview was at an end. "I do not know what your gentleman told you, but he has done us both a disservice in sending you here."

"Beggin' yer ledeyship's pardon. Yer' needful of one oo c'n bring th' girls up to snuff roit quick." She winked again. "An' that's whur I c'n he'p ye, so's we both line our purses wi' th' gold gent'men'll pay for the prime article."

The suggestion made it difficult for Sarah to draw a breath. "I believe you are labouring under a misconception," she said at last. Though she chose to appear unaffected by the ugly implication, a hot blush infused her features with furious colour. Striding to the door, she jerked it open and said, "We have nothing more to discuss."

Maggie Turpin stuck out her chin and planted both fists on her hips. "Much good it'll do ye to ride sich a high horse wi' me, mum."

"You are in no position to engage in threats," Sarah commanded. "Will you go?"

"Go?" She folded her arms over her stomach defiantly. "When I c'n tell ye oo 'twere gave me yer d'rection?"

"I would be grateful if you did," Sarah said, without softening her stiff reserve.

"Ow gradeful, mum?" She put out a hand, her fingers waggling enticingly.

141

Sarah shuddered. This person was nothing more than a vulture! Lifting her chin to its most disdainful height, she demanded, "Do you expect me to pay you?"

"Wush y'ou'd. A foin pickle I'd be in, living by me wits as I do, if I gaight away, afore I get me due."

Mentally reviewing the contents of her reticule, which included the muslin handkerchief with raspberry stain, a pair of crystal drop earrings, a vial of cologne, and a tin of lemon drops, but not a single coin of the realm, Sarah decided her best strategy was a prudent attack. She closed the door without latching it and moved towards the smug-faced intruder. "You are barking up the wrong tree, Miss Turpin, if you think you'll see one penny pass from my purse into your hand."

"Then me chaffer is sealed." Maggie drew her forefinger along her lips as though spreading sealing wax across them.

"I do not care in the least who set you up on this fool's errand. But if you persist in your odious threats and innuendo, I shall have you brought before the authorities."

"Na-ow don't be carryin' on so, me ledey," came the almost amused retort. "They got nothin' on Maggie Turpin."

"Perhaps not yet," Sarah allowed. "However, I'm certain Mr. Townshend and his Runners will find something for which you are culpable."

"I ain't never culped in me loife," Maggie protested. "I'm a workin' girl . . . ."

Sarah advanced upon her. "Then do not think I shall be your cat's paw. I won't be hoaxed or milked, Miss Turpin. Your intrusion into this household can be construed as nothing more than harassment." She paused for breath while Maggie's mouth opened and closed like a netted codfish. Then, before she could regain the power of speech, Sarah added, "You may go now. But if you return here, or create difficulties in an attempt to 'get your due,' I can promise you, you will earn nothing but trouble."

Suddenly the door flew open. Sarah's stern countenance swept from her cowardly visitor towards the newcomer.

"What's this?" demanded the Earl. "Mabb said there'd be trouble."

"Good day, My Lord," Sarah replied, not a little put out that her godmother's servants thought her so unable to take care of herself. "Sorry to inconvenience you. Miss Turpin is just leaving." With the introduction out of the way, she returned her gaze on Maggie.

"My lord," Maggie implored. "Tell 'er she'd best listen to me."

"It will do you no good to appeal to the Earl," Sarah said. "Your business here was with me, and I have told you we are at an end. Be so kind as to take yourself away now. Unless you wish to plead your case before a court of law."

Beneath Sarah's steel-coloured stare, Maggie seemed to be struggling against violent emotions. Then shrugging her shoulders as though she were bowing to a greater power, she said, "I'll go, me ledey. But ye'll be sorry ye were so soon shut o' me."

"It remains to be seen who will be sorry," Sarah said firmly. "Good day, Miss Turpin."

The blowsy brunette strutted out of the book room, her nose held high as if she were a high-born lady making an offended exit. When she left and Edward had gone after her, Sarah breathed a calming sigh and placed herself in a chair.

Upon returning to the library, he said, "I never would have thought it of you." He leaned his arms against the back cushion of the chair opposite Sarah's.

"That is absurd," Sarah said, wondering if everyone thought her so innocent of the ways of the world. "I daresay it would be very poor spirited in me to be forever asking others to give notice to incompetent servants or to reprimand an unruly student. One must be able to turn off troublesome individuals, after all."

"But what prompted you to see such a person in the first place?" he enquired, as he restlessly tapped the back of the chair with an open palm.

"My godmother told me several individuals had called about the school. I was in hopes . . . "

"That another Mrs. Chitham would present herself?" he said with a grin that lighted up her eyes.

"I . . . yes," she confessed. "Or that among the callers might have been one or two ladies willing to support the school for a year." She raised her shoulders in a disappointed shrug.

"Why do you not ask my mother?" he enquired as he came around the chair and placed himself in it.

"Oh no, I could not. She has given me so much already; t'would seem ungrateful, especially when her hopes differ from mine."

"I see," he said in a thoughtful manner. Rubbing his thumb over the curved armrest, he appeared to be considering a thorny problem. Then, smiling, he said, "You seem to be at odds with everyone who is concerned for you."

Sarah hastened to reassure him. "I wish you will not concern yourself. I have every reason to hope. After all, my predicament is not so unusual. Ladies are seldom credited with having serious interests."

"Forgive my bluntness, but you do not present the appearance of one with a serious thought in her head," he teased, bestowing an appreciative glance that did not fail to make her smile.

However his approving gaze pleased, she could not help agreeing with his point. "That is exactly what I mean, Dash. To be fitted out in pink and white like a green girl. I daresay the Bishop might have thought me more eligible if Mr. Godwyn had been able to report upon my sober and modest appearance."

He began to laugh. "I have my doubts, Sarah. Your unconscious habit of turning pink would make the most somber bombazine shine."

Saying, "Thank you, My Lord," Sarah darted a surprised glance at him and raised her hand to a cheek that was becoming disconcertingly warm beneath his intense gaze.

What did he mean? Did he suspect she was the Sparkler? Not knowing what to think, she wondered if friends caused one to feel like a top spinning off-balance. Only when one did not wish merely to be friends. What was she to do?

What was the matter with her? Pemberton was infatuated with a crystal illusion; enough so, her godmother thought, to advertise a *rendezvous* in a pleasure garden. That ought to tell her he thought the Sparkler no lady, but a demi-rep, a woman who delighted in such assignations. She was not gratified to feel a quiver of excitement, anticipating their meeting tomorrow evening.

He was watching her with a calm intensity which was all the more disconcerting because of the direction her thoughts had taken. As his grin warmed, she could almost imagine he was reading her mind. "I wish you will excuse me," she said, moving to the door. "I . . . have an appointment . . . a fitting."

"Are you making a purchase in scholarly black?" he enquired with a grin that was at once infatuating and endearing.

"No," she replied. "I have had enough of black."

"Then by all means, keep your appointment," he said, placing her in the care of her abigail. "You cannot know how lowering it is to engage a serious-looking lady in conversation."

When Sarah left Pemberton House, accompanied by a smug-faced Trent, she did not present the appearance of one keeping an appointment with her dressmaker. She was heavily veiled, and travelled not in Lady Pemberton's barouche, but in a hired carriage. She was immediately escorted to the owner of the palatial townhouse on Clarges Street, the venerable Mr. King of moneylenders. The urbane gentleman made her feel as comfortable as anyone meeting with the necessity of borrowing funds might be expected to feel in the presence of the one on whom all hopes now depend. He listened sympathetically to her plans, and she was considerably heartened when he voiced concern for her situation and expressed an interest in her ambition. "You are one of a few clients who do not propose to use the funds to repay another debt," he said approvingly. "This is the kind of transaction I like to make."

"I hope so sir," she said. Feeling the warmth of another blush colouring her cheeks, she was quick to add, "And I hope you will like it better in a year when I repay you."

"Ah, yes," he said, leaning his forearm on the elegantly embroidered armrests of his chair. "The infamous date of settlement. I think I can safely assume we have not done business before."

"No, sir. My father has had dealings with moneylenders, but I . . . "

"Quite wisely you have steered clear," he concluded.

"I would not be here now, if I did not have such faith in my calling."

She saw the glimmer of amusement crinkle the corners of his eyes. But instead of laughing, he merely said, "You will forgive me if I ask for more tangible proof of your good intentions."

"Of course, sir." Nervously Sarah twisted the handkerchief in her hands. "I had hoped you would take a mortgage on my property, just for a year."

"That is my usual mode of business, Miss. Do you have the deed?"

"No. My solicitor has it. But he has assured me Fair Meadow is unencumbered by debt."

"There is a reason for that, Miss," came the patient reply. After a moment's consideration, which Sarah knew better than to think was a hesitation, he explained, "The terms of your father's will were such that you may not mortgage the property or dispose of it in any manner without your solicitor's consent."

Beneath her veil, Sarah's shoulders slumped. "Oh. I didn't know. Mr. Quoinby posed no objections when I suggested I might sell."

"I would advise against doing that," he said soothingly. "You would be reduced to living on a restricted allowance."

"How do you know?" she enquired accusingly.

"It is my business to know," he replied, tapping his forehead. "Don't make many mistakes. Making a mortgage for you would be a mistake." He shrugged, as though regretting that business did not always go the way one wished. "Now, if you had any family jewels, I would feel safe in sending you to Howard & Gibbs."

"If I had jewels I would have gone to that establishment," she responded. "All I have is my land. Which I learn is useless to me."

He chuckled. "Not useless, I daresay. Merely entailed."

"I am not certain I am comfortable having you know so much about me," Sarah confessed, tugging on her gloves in preparation to leave.

"It would be the same wherever you went," he replied. "Solomon knows everything, as do Howard, Gibbs, Hamlet and Rundell. Do not waste your time asking them for money, Miss. They will give you the same advice." He rose and bowed. "I regret we cannot do business. Education is a fine thing."

She sighed heavily. "Thank you Mr. King. But it begins to appear as though there will be no school."

He shook his head regretfully. "So little faith. What will it hurt if you are compelled to delay opening your school a year or two? Nothing," he asserted. "In a year, you will have convinced the Bishop of your maturity, found a committee of ladies who will lend respectability to your scheme of educating deserving young women, and with their endorsement, you will have wealthy cits clamouring to place their daughters in your school."

"There is nothing wrong with your logic, sir," Sarah said. "Except that my aunt has hopes of establishing her elder daughter in my home before the year is out."

"You must have something to say about that," Mr. King said in a speculative manner. "I believe you will find the perfect means of financing your school, and silencing your critics."

Behind the veil, Sarah blushed again as she suggested, "You mean marriage."

"You are an intelligent woman," he said with a gently reproving smile; "I hope not so intelligent as to think yourself above the touch of affectionate bonds."

"No, I should like it above all things," she confessed. "Only at six-and-twenty, I must appear ridiculous if I were to look for a knight in shining armor to rescue me from my difficulties."

"Yes, well," Mr. King counselled as he summoned a footman to escort Miss Fairchild and her abigail to their conveyance. At the door, he said in a thoughtful manner, "It is to be hoped you do not refuse your 'knight' out of pride."

"He's right, Miss," said Trent, when they were again seated in the hired coach. " 'Pride goeth before the fall.' "

"Don't be absurd, Trent."

"Never more serious," replied the abigail. "You refused the Earl out of pride; don't make the same mistake again."

"Again? Do you expect me to accept just any proposal?"

"At least say you'll consider the next one," was Trent's suggestion.

Sarah laughed. "Very well, Trent. I shall consider the next proposal." Then, in a barely audible voice, she added, "Assuming there is one."

= 12 =

THOUGH SHE HAD hoped to ponder her dilemma in some privacy, her cousins and their escorts were awaiting her in Lady Pemberton's rose salon. "Are we actually to see the tarantula?" Chloe exclaimed upon Sarah making her entrance.

"If you wish to," she replied, thinking wearily that her younger cousin waxed more childlike each year. Chloe was clinging in apparently horrified anticipation to the arm of an officer of the Horse Guard—her Major Brown, Sarah assumed. The dark-haired warrior quietly spoke a few words into his effervescent lady's ear, when she coloured delicately and said, "I promise I will not faint, if you are with me, Niel."

"There can be no objection," Phoebe chimed in, though she had affected a tone more defensive than cajoling. "The Baron assured me the monster clatters like a wind-up toy, which is, of course, what it is." Her mustachioed hero was puffing out his barrel-shaped chest, although his preening stance made his stays creak. "Philip is very scientific," she enthused, rolling her hazel-coloured eyes at him in an adoring fashion. "He could, without a doubt, easily explain the workings of the tarantula."

"Now, Phoebe." He was wagging a finger at her in a gently reproving manner. "I cannot expect others to attend so faithfully upon my every word as do you."

"I have heard you are a scientific farmer," Sarah commented.

"Oh, he is," Phoebe offered. "Cawfield is a model plantation."

"Merely a matter of good management," he interjected.

149

"Anyone could do as well, using my methods. But I will not bore our friends with a technical monologue."

At that moment, Mr. Repton was admitted to the party, and having been apprised of the Baron's interest in modern farming, made enquiries which recommended him to the Baron as "a man of insight and progressive principles."

In an affable manner, Mr. Repton wished the Baron might lend his expertise to Miss Fairchild. "It occurs to me your techniques might improve her crop yield, which would ease her worries considerably."

"I did not know you were interested in farming," she said as the party adjourned to the carriage which was to convey the ladies to the Museum.

"Yes, it is an ambition of mine," he said diffidently. "However I must limit my study to theory, as I have not yet acquired the right parcel of land." As he was handing her into the barouche, he bestowed such a speaking gaze upon her, she was compelled to look away. Then she saw Lord Pemberton in the library window, staring at her escort with a jealous look. Before she took her place in the carriage, she caught his eye, and was stunned by the fevered enquiry therein. After a moment, he turned aside as though the sight of her caused him considerable pain. Sarah was left to think herself with no hope of lightening his heavy heart. All anticipation of the expedition dissolved, but she realised she could not disappoint the others by suddenly quitting the party. Settling uneasily against the cushion, she made an effort to attend to her cousins' spritely exchange with their escorts whose mounts were prancing alongside the moving vehicle. The ladies were advancing the scheme of immediately viewing Week's mechanical spider against the Major and the Baron's concerted opposition. Sarah maintained a silent vigil in her corner of the barouche, until Phoebe made an appeal to her. "We shall let Sarah judge what we must first see," she was saying and looking expectantly in her direction.

"I have no opinion," Sarah asserted. "Indeed, Cousin, you

and Chloe must come to an agreement with Baron Cawford and Major Brown, or we shall be obliged to see nothing."

Mr. Repton, astride a spirited chestnut, chuckled. "I hope you do not expect your students to settle disputes by themselves."

Surprised, Sarah replied, "It would be impertinent for me to tell my grown cousins how to resolve disagreements, Mr. Repton. If I decided with them, you might justly accuse me of taking their side because we are women. If I sided against them, they would pout and do their utmost to spoil the day." She nodded approvingly. "You see, they have already made peace with their adversaries." Phoebe and her sister were fluttering fans and eyelashes at the Baron and the Major who promised they might see the disputed exhibit after they had taken in another gallery. "Then I shall make no complaint if the spider frightens you out of all proportion to its size," the Baron was saying with a cautionary lift of his thick brown eyebrows.

When they were set down before the Museum doors, the majority of the party declared themselves satisfied with the compromise, although Chloe was still pouting, in an attempt, Sarah thought, to soften Major Brown's determination against seeing the mechanical tarantula so soon in the expedition. As he was handing her out of the carriage, Sarah overheard him issue a silken command. "Smile, my dear, and stop sulking, or I shall take you home, and there will be no spider for you."

"But Niel," she began in a cajoling tone.

"I pray you do not try me on this, Chloe," he was saying. "My patience is at an end."

"Oh, very well," she replied. "You needn't treat me like a child."

"Then don't act like one," he countered firmly, drawing her out of the way, when Sarah took Mr. Repton's hand to step onto the curb.

The admission being paid, they consulted the guidebook to map out the best assault on the Museum. In this discussion, the three ladies played no part, two of them glancing with wide-eyed wonder in the direction from which echoed startled shrieks and laughter, while Sarah confessed herself willing to see as many exhibits as the gentlemen thought they might view before taking the main attraction.

While they were strolling through the hall which housed a variety of mechanical birds which chirped and warbled so naturally, Sarah began to wonder whether the Baron might not have mistaken the tarantula's realism. Mr. Repton drew her a little apart from their companions who were clustered before a trilling nightingale. "Did the Bishop grant you funds for your school?" he enquired.

"No," she confessed. "I have not exhausted my resources, but I must own I am sadly discouraged."

"Not you," he answered, consulting his guidebook. "You have met with a setback." Sarah found herself unable to evade his suddenly too intense stare. She felt like one of the mechanical birds singing in its cage, though she could not have explained her uneasiness. His consideration was all that was proper, and he broke their gaze before she could say it was the root of her discomfiture. He was considering a meadowlark which was valiantly flapping its wings as though making an attempt to escape the display, when he announced, "I think I may have discovered a way to fund your seminary."

"I told you, I cannot accept your . . . " she said feebly.

"Will you listen?" he demanded, urgently turning towards her. Sarah's eyes fluttered to his, enabling her to witness his struggle to master his emotions. "This is neither the time nor place," he said at last. "Will you allow me a few moments to explain?"

"Yes, of course, at my godmother's home," she replied, moving nervously towards her cousins who were hurrying their escorts towards the main hall.

"Please, Miss Fairchild," he said, in a halting fashion. "Will you allow me to drive you in the park this afternoon?"

"Mr. Repton, I, . . . " she began glancing after their

companions who seemed oblivious that they were leaving her behind.

"If you will be more comfortable, you must bring your abigail," he said. Laughing a little, he confessed, "I know the World will not credit me with wanting to do an honourable thing."

"Then do not ask me to drive with you," she replied.

"Very well I shall call at Pemberton House," he said in a fervent manner. Leading her towards their company who were at that moment making their entrance into the tarantula's lair, he made no other comment, but applied himself to making her comfortable with the sight they were about to witness, that Sarah began to feel some trepidation.

"I am not one of those vapid fools," she insisted, to bolster her flagging courage "who fall into convulsions when they see a spider on the wall."

"I am sure you are no coward when it comes to murdering spiders," he assured her. "But this is no garden variety insect, dear lady." He was encompassing with his hands a circle of no smaller than six inches. "I think it must eat slippers to whet its appetite." Laughing, he waggled his fingers in a manner very like the menacing dance of a spider dangling from its silk.

Her grey eyes opened wide in awe. Then, laughing at her involuntary jitters, she playfully tapped his fingers. "Really, Mr. Repton. We are discussing a mechanical toy; not the bloodthirsty Minotaur."

"Ah, yes, but this toy takes on a hideous life of its own; a life dedicated to avenging the heedless deaths of its smaller brothers. . . . "

"Sisters," Sarah corrected, giggling.

"You are too scientific," he chided, teasingly. "But if you will have it so, sisters. A matter of honour to defend one's sisters." He impelled her towards their party. Chloe and Phoebe were suddenly hanging back, as though their courage had entirely failed them.

Sarah was unable to stem her enjoyment of the danger

into which Mr. Repton was thrusting her. "What's this?" she enquired, turning upon him. "Mr. Repton, are you hiding behind my skirt?"

"Not a'tall," he protested gaily. "Merely the rear guard."

As they passed into the room housing the tarantula, Chloe uttered an ear-splitting shriek before falling in a dead faint in front of the skittering machine. A frisson of dread fingered Sarah's spine as she rushed to her cousin's aid. Major Brown was alternately applying her vinaigrette and patting her pale cheeks. "Chloe," he cried, seemingly as stricken as if he had seen a brother in arms fall in battle.

"Calm yourself, Major," Sarah soothed as she took the bottle of smelling salts from his hand. "She is overwrought. Kindly remove her from the room, and she will revive."

"Are you certain?" he enquired, turning a wild-eyed look upon her.

"Beyond a doubt, sir." As he lifted his delicate burden, Sarah said, "You must continue to be firm with her, Major. Do not let her rule you with her vapours."

By this time, Phoebe had added her voice to the general hubbub in the gallery. "You were mistaken, Philip," she said, almost severely. "The tarantula is truly hideous. I cannot take my eyes from it. Ooh!" She hid her eyes against the Baron's sturdy shoulder and trembled until his arm folded around her. "Oh, why did I not listen to you? Take me from this place," she said, shuddering in a manner which must convince all who knew her that she was a lady of sensibility. As the Baron obliged her trembling cousin, Sarah turned to regard the terrible tarantula which was skittering about its enclosure. "Oh, it is so ugly," she cried breathlessly. Phoebe was not exaggerating when she said she could not look away. But Sarah was not repulsed by its seemingly intelligent wanderings. "How does it work?"

"Philosopher's stone?" suggested Mr. Repton.

"Certainly you do not believe in sorcery," she chided, taking her eyes from the clattering arachnid to tease her companion.

"Not I," he replied, grinning. "I have never yet lost my reason. Have you seen enough?"

"Yes," she said, looking over her shoulder at the retreating tarantula as she was guided towards the door. "Only I wish I might study its mechanism."

"Well, you cannot," Mr. Repton said in a quelling tone immediately prior to rejoining the rest of their party.

Sarah chose to ignore his possessive manner, but turned to Chloe, who, seated upon a bench in the wide hallway, was assuring Major Brown that she had indeed recovered from her fright.

"Good, then I shall take you home," he was informing her. When she made as if to protest her eagerness to make another attempt to view the dreadful creature, he insisted as he supported her weight on an arm, "I wish you will say no more about this spider. You have no more sense than a child. Indeed, I have no doubt you will suffer nightmares tonight."

"She will," Phoebe volunteered disparagingly. "And if I get no sleep on your account, Miss, you shall hear about it."

"I wish you will not peck at Chloe," Sarah interjected, seeing how dangerously pale her cousin's complexion had become. "Major Brown, you must take her home immediately. We will hire a coach to deliver us to Pemberton House."

"Sarah!" exclaimed Phoebe. "You cannot mean to suggest Chloe ride home unaccompanied."

"She meant nothing of the sort," Baron Cawford soothed. "Miss Fairchild is entirely correct in sending Chloe home in the care of the Major. But we cannot leave your cousin unchaperoned." He rolled a mistrustful eye over Sarah's escort.

"By no means," Repton was agreeing. "Her good name means the world to me."

"And what about my sister's respectability?" Phoebe demanded, her plump fingers clenched into fists at the side of her apricot-coloured muslin skirt.

"Oh, do be quiet, Phoebe!" Chloe insisted shakily. "Major Brown and I are engaged; I will not listen to you or anyone else impugn him."

Her colour was returning rapidly, Sarah noted, growing more easy in her mind. "Congratulations, Major." She embraced her trembling cousin. "I wish you happy, dear. Let us all leave now; Chloe is much better, and we have reason to celebrate."

But Phoebe was not of the same opinion. "How could you?" she hissed into her sister's ear in an affected whisper that Sarah easily overheard. "You know Mama wants me to marry first."

"I cannot wait for you to tie the knot," Chloe hissed back defensively, before turning back to her fiancé. "We have been apart six years, and in all that time Mama has been badgering me not to wear my heart upon my sleeve." Smiling tremulously, she gazed at her tall officer and said as he handed her into the carriage, "I shall tie it on with ribbons, Niel, so everyone knows I love you."

He patted her little hand and said smilingly, "Just make sure I know, dear."

She was blushing becomingly when Sarah climbed into the conveyance, satisfied her younger cousin had been well-matched in Major Brown. Even Cousin Phoebe, nursing her irritation, seemed well-suited to the stolid Baron Cawford. He was drawing her out of her pet with a seemingly oblivious monologue on the inner workings of the tarantula, a confusing and pedantic discourse on gears and levers and mainsprings which seemed nevertheless to animate Phoebe out of the glumps. "Oh, Philip, you have such a head," she said adoringly. "I never cease to be amazed."

"Yes, well, I do go on," he owned, his ruddy face turning darker. "Beg pardon, all. Can't help m'self."

When they had set Phoebe, the Baron, Chloe and Major Brown down in Hanover Square, Mr. Repton accompanied Sarah to the door of Pemberton House. During the whole of the short drive, he was curiously attentive, reminding her of his wish to support her, and repeatedly saying that he had been particularly impressed by her courage at Week's Museum. Remembering Lady Blake's vague warnings, Sarah took his effusive compliments with a grain of salt. When she reached her godmother's home, she bounded down from the barouche, very nearly into Repton's waiting arms. As she disengaged herself, her eyes darted towards the window wherein she had seen Edward on their departure. It was unoccupied. Breathing a sigh of relief, she said all that was proper without being too encouraging, and began to run up the steps. But as she turned to go, he caught her hand in his and pressed a kiss upon her wrist. "Mr. Repton," she said reproachfully, withdrawing her fingers from his fervent grasp, and pressing them protectively against her bosom. "Good day."

"It has been," he said. "I hope I may wish you a more satisfying evening."

Thinking he was referring to his plans for her school, she thanked him, then entered the house. Tossing her bonnet and gloves on the gilt gesso table in the front hall, she made a beeline for the library. Edward looked up from a copy of the Gentleman's Magazine and said grudgingly, "You look happy."

"I am, I think," she replied, thumping down on a chair at his elbow. "The tarantula was truly wonderful." Kicking off a shoe, she curled her feet beneath her on the cushion; then, pouting her lips, said, "You look anything but happy."

"Yes, well, I cannot like the company you kept," he said, returning his gaze upon his periodical.

"You cannot mean my cousins," she enquired lightly as she twirled a lock of hair around her finger. When he did not reply, she looked up at him. He seemed to be in a trance; his gaze arrested upon the shoe still dangling from her toe. If she didn't know he was consumed with passion for the Sparkler, she would have thought him hungry for herself, especially as he licked his lips like a starveling.

The unconscious motion seemed to awaken him. "Your cousins?" he said as though from a great distance, then severely, "No, I think you take my meaning."

"Yes, you refer to Mr. Repton." She leaned an elbow upon the drum table that separated them and confided, "Surely you can have no objection to his interest in setting up my school."

He regarded her as though he thought she had as much experience in the world as did the duckling he had called her last night, then said, "If you knew him better, you too would suspect his interest. I would steer clear of whatever offer of support he makes you, Sarah."

He was jealous. The realisation made her wonder whether Edward cared more for her than he had let on. What had he said the other evening: his feelings were real? Was it possible he had been talking about his concern for her and not simply his craving for an unknown Sparkler? The possibility made her happier than she had been in ages. Still, having made no serious overtures himself—for she would not credit his odious proposal on the road in Huntingdon—he had no right to dictate whom she received.

"I'm for tea," she said, coming to her feet and moving towards the door. Before departing the book room, she half-turned and regarded him. "Do you want anything?"

He reached for the Post which was folded over the arm of his chair, shaking his head no and saying, "Nothing, thank you." Watching her pad in stocking feet out of the room, he thought it a good sign that she had an appetite. At least her stomach did not seem to be in love with Charles Repton. Lighter in mood, he shook open the newspaper, wondering whether they had gotten his advertisement printed properly.

His eyes went right away to the notice which began "To the Sparkler." Had she read this lurid invitation? Why, he wondered, had she not called on him? Crumpling the paper, he flung himself out of the chair and began pacing the floor. Damn, damn, and damn. He imagined the entire readership of the Post secreting themselves along the infamous dark walks to command a view of the Sparkler's seduction.

How many other fools had she wrapped around her little finger, he fumed. Rummaging through the pages, he found only one other advertisement—his. In the back of the paper, between two notices—one for the liquidation of an estate, the other a husband's search for his runaway wife. If that weren't enough to fry his liver. Situated as it was, his notice "To an Unknown Lady," was virtually invisible. It was inconceivable to think she would meet him tomorrow morning during his customary ride in Green Park.

=== 13 ===

RETIRING TO HIS room to dress for dinner, Edward was informed Nigglesworth was awaiting him with news. He was admitted at once into the Earl's chambers, where as he jerked off his broad-brimmed hat, he was rewarded with a tankard of ale prior to beginning to recount his adventures of the day.

Attired in a forest green dressing gown, Edward sat patiently in his armchair, knowing his groom would open his budget in his own good time. To set his groom at ease in the uncommonly elegant surroundings—the mahogany panelled walls, Persian carpeted floor and overlarge furnishings—the Earl occasionally sipped from his own glass of stout, until Nigglesworth, perched stiffly upon the edge of a chair, had quaffed a goodly portion of his refreshment. At last the short man wiped his mouth with a hand and ran it through his wild, grey hair; the signal Edward took to mean he was ready to launch into his tale.

"Thankee, me lord," Nigglesworth began, setting the tankard on the silver tray which reposed on a pedestal table. After rubbing the palms on his trousers, he rested both large hands on his knees. "I own the Turpin led me a merry chase, but I never lost hide nor hair ov'er, though in faith I near went off at side. Stopped in every shop on Monmouth Street, 'cept the ale houses, worse luck."

Edward chuckled. Despite his groom's apparently aimless recitation, he knew he would eventually make a point worth hearing. "You seem to have been treated to a day which was the envy of any young lady with pin money."

"I don't know 'bout that, me lord." Nigglesworth coughed into his hand. "As I sen, her jaunterin' near had me pullin' out me hure."

Being accustomed to his employee's long-winded accounts, Edward was in no wise near to pulling out his own thick hair. Still, he knew that unless he trimmed the yarn, he was destined for a street by street report. "Did Miss Turpin show her true colours at last?"

"Aye, me lord. She did. Passed time wi' several gents. After which," Nigglesworth, blushing to the roots of his sparse hair, "her purse hung a little heavier on 'er belt."

Edward's irrepressible grin widened. He folded an arm over the corner of his chair's backrest as he taxed his man. "For shame, Nigglesworth; you don't strike me as the sort of fellow who'd eavesdrop on a private conversation."

"My orders were to follow the wench, an' tell ye what I saw." Grinning, he raised his hands from his knees and, splaying them before himself in an arresting motion, said, "But, if I've offended, I'll say no more."

"Go on," Edward urged, pouring Nigglesworth another ration. "When did you ever stop your prattle on account of what I thought?"

"Never, me lord," Nigglesworth said, grinning after downing a goodly portion of his drink. As if confident of his master's good will, he continued, "Since ye give me leave, I'll open my budget." Clearing his throat, he took another pull from his tankard. "Maggie Turpin'd take blunt from Owd-nick, hisse'f, i'n 'e 'ad a mind to please 'er."

"What's that to our purpose?" Edward persisted. "Who did Maggie take money from?"

Nigglesworth stretched his bandy legs towards the cold fireplace. "Nobody I knowed at first; a couple of Johnny Raws, and a spindle-shanked deacon; least I thought he was, on account of his crow's weeds." At this, he shook his head, as if regretting the sorry state of the world.

Edward choked back laughter as he made the charitable

suggestion. "Very probably the good man was contemplating her spiritual health."

Nigglesworth darted a needling look at his employer. "I'n 'e was, his sermon didn't take, sir. She entertained two more gents, before another gentleman took 'er up in his curricle."

"Our Maggie seems to have had quite a profitable day," Edward marvelled. "I suppose you lost her then."

"Did not," Nigglesworth insisted. "The gentleman tied off 'is team, and they took themse'ves into a house on Brewer Street.'

"Did you perchance recognise this gentleman?" Edward enquired, hoping his groom wasn't preparing to lead him down a blind alley.

"Better you sh'd ask i'n he knew me," retorted the groom obstinately. "Never worry, sir, I was careful 'e din't clap his peepers on me. Sure an' I knew 'im. Hasn't 'e been shadowin' Miss Fairchild for the week an' more?"

Edward's fingers clutched the arm rests as he pushed himself to his feet. "Never tell me it was Charles Repton."

"One and the same, me lor'," Nigglesworth replied smugly.

"Blast." Edward collapsed into his chair, and, cupping a hand around his mouth and chin, fell into an ominous silence.

"Well you might sen it, me lord. 'E was in no good mood when Turpin took 'er leave, I can tell you, though she was wearin' a grin like the cat wot got the canary. Think she plucked 'im good," he said chuckling.

"Better him than me," Edward finally said with a hard grin. Placing two gold sovereigns into his groom's hand, he added, "You've earned your vale today. Thank you."

"Well, I ain't one to take more than is due me, sir, seein's how it 'pears Mr. Repton is playin' fast an' loose wi' yer lady." Then, throwing back his head, Nigglesworth drained his mug as if to celebrate his devotion to duty, then replacing his hat, took himself away while Edward smilingly contemplated his groom's unconscious assumption that Sarah was his lady.

Swathed in apricot-coloured and white striped silk, Sarah awaited Mr. Repton in Lady Pemberton's blue salon. Trent, seated in a nearby chair, was attending to French work in an unobtrusive but observant manner, to lend countenance to this meeting, despite Sarah's insistence that nothing could be more harmless than the reason he had asked her to receive him—her school.

Stabbing the white muslin with her needle, Trent said, "And so it will be, with me here to keep him harmless, Miss." When Sarah folded her hands in her lap, Trent suggested, "Why do you not play something on the pianoforte. Unless you'd rather the gentleman think you have nothing to do but wait on him."

Since she was not at all desirous of having Mr. Repton think her dangling for him, Sarah adjourned to the instrument and began to rehearse a sonata by Mozart. While she was playing, she realized Mr. Repton had been admitted to the salon, but she persisted in playing until the piece was at an end, lest her abigail accuse her of being overanxious to begin the interview.

"Very nice," he said, applauding as she closed the keyboard. "Do you also sing?"

"I number the usual feminine accomplishments among my talents," she said, offering him a chair opposite the one in which she placed herself. "I intend the young ladies who will be attending my school will not lack for opportunities to develop their artistic talents."

"Miss Fairchild," he said, leaning forwards in his chair, as though to share a confidence. "I did not come to review your curriculum."

But my backers will wish to know what I plan to teach the girls," she protested.

"I am confident you will know precisely what they must learn," he said in such an intense tone, that Trent looked up from her embroidery.

His urgency raised an instinctive warning flag within Sarah's sensitive brain. She felt compelled to say, "Then you are alone in your confidence, sir. And I am surprised you have discovered a committee willing to risk everything on a green girl."

He rubbed his lower lip, then caught her gaze in his startling blue stare. "Sarah, I have considered every possibility, and I must tell you, I see no way for you to open a school this year."

"But you said you knew a way," she began hesitantly.

"There is only one possibility," he replied, coming to his feet to pace the floor in a thoughtful manner. "You are a strong-willed woman; I have my doubts that certain parties will support your ambition, fearing you will encourage your charges to cultivate what they might call willfulness."

She nodded her head thoughtfully. "That may be part of their reluctance. But I fully intend to teach the skills vital to managing a large household and the graces necessary to advancing in Society."

He turned on his heel and facing her, tapped his chest, "*I* am convinced. But others are harder nuts to crack."

"Please do not leave me in suspense, Mr. Repton," Sarah said with another shake of her head. "How can I convince these pillars of society of my stability?"

Moving towards her, he said carefully, "There is a way to suppress their doubts. If you were married, their suspicions must be laid to rest."

She gave a little start and laughed, causing the ringlets, which Trent had taken such pains to make appear naturally contrived, to shimmer and dance. "I beg your pardon, sir? You have caught me napping. Did you suggest marriage?"

As though charmed by her artless response, he leaned towards her. "You did not mishear me, Sarah. You cannot find a benefactor among the Church, and ladies seem to believe you unequal to the task. It is the only way," he said, flashing a sensual smile that, Sarah knew, was intended to make her heart skip beats.

Indeed, her heart had seemed to stop a moment ago, but at this moment, it was tripping along quite unaffectedly. She moistened her lips and quipped, "Who is to be the sacrificial lamb, Mr. Repton?"

"This levity will not serve," he replied in a suddenly severe tone which only increased her misgivings. "You must know your situation is precarious at best."

"You are not the first to tell me I need a husband to advance in my calling," she said.

"But I am, I hope, the first to make such an offer," he said, taking her hand in his. Sarah attempted to withdraw her fingers, but he continued in a mollifying tone, "Don't take umbrage, Sarah. I admire your independence; indeed I should do nothing to moderate it."

"But I do not love you," she protested, finally winning her hand back.

"Neither do I love you," he replied bluntly. "But each of us is in possession of that which the other desires. I have money with which to fund your school, and you have . . . standing which will solidify my position in Society."

"You make it sound so . . . mercenary," Sarah said uncomfortably. She glanced at her abigail who was staring at her as if silently urging her to say she'd at least consider the match.

"Most marriages are rather mercenary," he said. "But only consider; would a marriage in name only be so hard for you to bear, if it would enable you to realise your dream?"

He presented such a charming appearance of boyish persuasion that Sarah reluctantly silenced the inner voice. Still, wanting convincing, she said, "You wish to make a convenient marriage. I do not understand why you chose me. I have nothing to bring you."

"You have everything I need," he replied. "You will lend me countenance in Society, and provide me with the means to become a landed gentleman. I hope" he said, moving nearer, "you will not long consider our marriage convenient. Please, say you will be my wife."

"I . . . ," Sarah turned from him, to keep her countenance from revealing her disappointment. He did not love her; he only wanted her land. But no alternative had presented itself to her. In fact, doors seemed to be slamming in her face. Sensibly, she knew herself to be foolish for her prejudice against him, but she would not accept his offer immediately. "I need time to consider your . . . very kind offer, Mr. Repton." She heard the snort of disdain Trent exhaled. How could she explain her aversion to a marriage which would be the means of achieving her own fondest hope?

"By all means, take time to consider," he said, smoothly withdrawing a step, as though conscious of the maidenly confusion which had left her bereft of speech. "I shall seek you out tomorrow evening, with the hope that you will make me the happiest of men." So saying he bowed himself out of the salon.

"What do you mean, you'll consider his offer?" Trent snapped, upon returning to the salon after assuring herself the Reprobate had left the establishment.

"Is that not what you were wishful for me to do?" Sarah replied. "Consider an offer of marriage?"

"Not with the likes of him, Miss. Do you know what he will do to your school?"

"He has assured me. . . . "

"Assurances mean nothing to a man of his ilk," Trent declared, her blue eyes narrowing in mistrust. "He wants to be master of Fair Meadow. And of you."

"Really, Trent, this is not the Dark Ages," Sarah scoffed. "What will he do, ruin me to keep me from opening the school?"

"Do you doubt your husband can deny you everything you hope for?"

"I know a wife's property becomes her husband's by law; but Trent, surely Mr. Repton will agree to a joint venture. Fair Meadow can be held in trust for my children."

"If you have children," Trent countered.

"Well, of course, if I marry, I hope I may have . . . "

Shaking her grey head, the older woman folded her arms across her frame. "You goose. Mr. Repton specified a marriage in name only. How do you propose you'll get children if he never visits your bed?"

Sarah turned away to conceal the hot colour that was flooding her face. If what Trent was saying was true, he felt no affection for her at all, but only offered her the sop of marriage because he needed her to gain a potentially profitable farm at no expense. Tears stung her eyelids as she dashed out of the salon. Did no one love her?

Blinded by tears, she ran into Edward's arms. "Here, what's this?" he enquired, handing her his handkerchief.

"Nothing, My Lord," she sniffed, when he had set her upon a bench in the hall. After dabbing at her eyes and nose, she balled the soft linen in her fist.

"Doesn't look like nothing," he said, seating himself beside her. Gently he took her hand in his. "Have you lost your last friend?"

She darted a newly tearful look in his direction, and said with trembling lips, "Never tell me you no longer wish to be my friend."

"Of course, I wish it above all things." He smoothed a golden curl into its hairpin. "Only you have not been treating me as your friend, Sarah."

"How have I not?"

"Friends confide in one another," he said, increasing her resemblance to a watering pot. Folding an arm around her shoulders, he let her cry against his chest. "Will you tell me why you are so unhappy?"

"I have received a proposal," she cried. "Only he wishes it to be a marriage in name only."

He smoothed his neck-cloth as though it was suddenly choking him. "I did not expect that," he said at last.

"Neither did I," she said into his waistcoat. "I want a real marriage, with children."

"Did you tell him?"

"How can I tell him I cannot accept his conditions if he will marry me?"

"Why do you wish to marry a man who will not . . . " His question faltered as he coughed into his hand.

"I need to marry. My school . . . " she shrugged, as if saying that her grief signified nothing.

"Well," he drawled, for want of anything to say. Then, rubbing a knot out of her little shoulder, he said, "You must insist upon having a real marriage."

"Can a wife make her husband love her?"

He squeezed her shoulder in a consoling manner. She was right. A married woman retained virtually no rights in the eyes of the law which recognised the man as the "one flesh" into which a man and woman joined in marriage. What could he say? 'Don't marry him?' That sounded more like a dog in the manger than advice of a concerned friend. He rubbed his scalp until he thought of a suitable reply. "Better to remain friends, Sarah," he said as lightly as he was able, given the agitation she had aroused within his breast.

"He will not be my friend," she said, twisting the linen square into a knot. "And he will not support my school unless I marry him."

"According to his conditions," he added, knowing without a doubt who her suitor had been. "Sarah, do you wish to be Rep's friend?"

She lifted her tearstreaked face from Edward's comforting chest to gaze into his dear eyes. Shaking her head no, she confessed, "No, I do not wish to be his friend."

Edward's pride demanded he bow to her desire. After all, he was not one to court an unwilling sweetheart. But, as he entrusted Sarah into the care of her abigail, and made himself ready to leave the house, he realised he was not one to stand aside when the woman he loved was about to travel down the garden path with a deceitful snake.

=== 14 ===

"WHAT CAN THIS letter mean?" demanded Lady Pemberton as she burst into her son's chamber.

The Earl, his chin elevated during the torturous process of tying his neck-cloth, glanced in the mirror at his mother who was standing behind him. She was tapping her satin-clad toe on the mahogany floor, impatiently awaiting his explanation, which, he regretted must wait upon the successful completion of his Waterfall. After what seemed an interminable length of time, while he fiddled with folds, he lowered his chin by degrees until he had achieved a perfect crease in the starched linen. Then, as his valet handed him into an exquisitely tailored coat of peacock green superfine, he turned to face her.

"I see you received Lady Blake's note," he replied.

Lady Pemberton shuddered delicately as though controlling a violent emotion. "I know who wrote it. Whose crack-brained idea is this?" She was slapping her folded fan against the paper in a manner reminiscent of a parent rapping knuckles.

Involuntarily, Edward clenched a fist behind his back. "It was my crack-brained idea, Mother," he said. How he wished she would leave him in peace. But she presented the clench-jawed appearance of one who would not leave without a full explanation.

Indeed, she enquired in a testy manner. "What does it mean? We must support Sarah's school?"

"*I* cannot do it, Mother," he said, his patience taxed to

the limit. "Even if it were proper for me to give Sarah the money for Fair Meadow, she would never take it."

"But Edward, I do not wish Sarah to teach. I want her to be married."

"Then do nothing, Mother, and she will marry Charles Repton," he said, guiding his mother to the door of his chamber.

"But why Charles?" she demanded, halting on the threshold. "When any fool with half a brain can plainly see it's you she loves."

Edward stopped in his steps. Sarah loved him? Then why did she not tell him? Why had she said she wished him to be her friend when he had come close to baring his soul to her last night?

He picked up his riding crop and accepted his hat from his silent valet who nodded as if confirming Lady Pemberton's assertion.

If Sarah loved him, why had she turned him down? "Go ask her yourself, Mother," he snapped. "It's beyond my meager comprehension."

"That I will never do," she said firmly. "As it would make her fly straight into his arms." He smacked the riding crop against his boot angrily. "Don't fly into a rage against me, Pemberton. None of this would have happened if *you* had told her *you* loved her."

Furiously he strode down the hall, leaving her sputtering fury which she was compelled to suppress as a maid haltingly informed her that Lady Blake was awaiting her ladyship in the rose salon.

Having received the same summons, Sarah met her dark-visaged godmother at the doorway. She allowed the older woman to precede her into the rose-papered chamber. Lady Pemberton shot a dagger-look at her. What had she done to earn such a dark frown, she wondered as she placed herself in an armless chair.

"Good morning, Elizabeth, Sarah," the Marchioness said enthusiastically, seemingly impervious to Lady Pemberton's furious stare. "I daresay this is an unfashionable hour to be making a call, but you, my dear," beaming at Sarah, "will not wish to delay this interview."

"Only if you are bringing me good tidings," she replied without blushing.

"Can you doubt it?" enquired the Lioness. "When your letter is the reason I have come?"

Lady Pemberton had endured this exchange in silence, but glaring at her goddaughter, she enquired, "Have you been pestering Letitia about your school?"

"Why should she not?" snapped that lady in reply. "*I* did not condemn her scheme at the outset."

The Countess sniffed an insulted breath. "I did not condemn her school."

"But neither did you promote it, by presenting your goddaughter so becomingly." Lady Blake indicated Sarah with a flourish of her ruby-studded hand. She was smoothing a wrinkle from the skirt of her blue sprig muslin morning dress that flared from a pleated bodice of the same fabric. White kid slippers peeped demurely beneath the skirt which ended in a flounce of vandyked lace. It was a becoming costume, but Lady Blake was correct in doubting its suitability to teaching. "Is that the garb of a serious-minded young woman?"

Lady Pemberton lowered her head as though she were ashamed of her handiwork. Then, raising her gaze, she said, "Letitia, please; I thought I had Sarah's best interest at heart."

"I daresay that is the lamest excuse for mistakes in judgement I have ever heard," roared the Lioness. "And the most common."

"But what have I done that is so terrible?" enquired Lady Pemberton.

"Really, Godmama, you have done nothing terrible," Sarah said to soothe her godmother's distress. "I do like my new dresses. . . . "

"Hush," demanded the Marchioness as she slammed the

tip of her walking stick into the floor, earning immediate and startled silence. "I daresay you know what you have wrought with your flounces and bows, Elizabeth. Before Sarah can be taken seriously in the *ton*, she must be married."

Sarah began to chew reflectively upon her lower lip. Perhaps it might be better if she should bow to worldly logic. "If I must be married before the *ton* will support my school, I can set your mind at rest."

"I wish you will," said the Lioness in a tone which suggested she doubted whether anyone could relieve her worried mind.

"Charles Repton has offered for me," Sarah explained, picking nervously at a cornflower which was appliqued on the skirt at her left knee.

"Is that the sort of information you think will ease my concern?" Lady Blake demanded, impatiently turning the silver-handled walking stick around so that its tip bore into Lady Pemberton's Persian carpet. "Do you listen to nothing I tell you? He is completely ineligible."

"I know," Sarah responded. "He has told me he has no family, save for one brother."

"Fustian," exploded the Marchioness. "Charles is my nephew; my younger sister's first child. She ran off with a gamester; family disowned her, but she and I corresponded through the years. I sent her son to Eton; promised I should set him up when he came of age. Being my relative does not recommend him to me—I know his character better than anyone. He is as ineligible as his father was."

Elizabeth leaned forwards, arresting the Marchioness's abuse of her rug, her eyebrows lifted deferentially when Lady Blake glared at her. "I do not know, Letitia. He is your relative; that will lend him countenance anywhere. And he is quite charming."

"Meaning he will have schoolgirls falling in love with him in every hallway," the Marchioness snapped. "Very convenient for him, I daresay."

"No he will not," Sarah declared, half coming to her feet.

"Of course he will not," agreed her godmother. "When he is a married man, his manner will change. Men always settle down when their honour is at stake."

In response to Lady Pemberton's assurance, the Lioness snorted in derision. "How naive you are, Elizabeth, and how fortunate that your husband lived up to your expectations. Sarah will not be as lucky if she marries my nephew. Charles has no understanding of the word honour." She held up a restraining hand when her companions gave voice to protests. "Believe me when I tell you this; you know how I dislike carrying tales. During his last year at Eton, how can I say the words? he seduced an innocent girl of fifteen, then abandoned her, though she was carrying his child."

"He could not be so cruel," interjected Lady Pemberton. "The poor child!"

"He did not care that she drowned herself rather than bear a child in shame." The Marchioness shook her head remorsefully. "I cannot tell you how many times I have lifted that poor soul, and her tormentor, in prayer. But it seems to run off him, like water off a duck's back."

"Why have you not disowned him?" demanded the Countess.

"He was in hopes that I should give him a large settlement, including property in Town and in Kent. However, he has proven his unworthiness over and again." Lady Blake gazed pointedly at Sarah. "That is why he is so keen to marry a lady of property."

"I own I was deceived in him," Sarah said, though the words came hard. "He has a silver tongue, which makes falsehoods ring true. But he will not come near the girls in my charge."

"My dear, Charles will do whatever he desires," Lady Blake scoffed. "You cannot think he will change his spots merely because he acquires a wife."

"You mistake my meaning, ma'am," Sarah insisted. She tapped a finger against her lips before continuing. "If I were to marry Mr. Repton, he would never allow my school to open. Or if he did encourage my hopes, I should deny myself. How could I ask parents to place their daughters into a household where he must reign supreme?" She gave her head a vehement shake. "No, I cannot be so unfeeling. I will not marry Charles Repton."

"That puts those fears to rest," said the Marchioness. "And now we can discuss the reason for my unfashionably early visit. I received your enquiry yesterday morning, spoke with Mr. Godwyn yesterday afternoon, and decided last night Elizabeth and I must endow your school."

"You decided?" interjected Lady Pemberton, and in considerable confusion, demanded of her goddaughter, "Why did you not ask for my help?"

Sarah embraced her. "You have given me so much already, Godmama; I thought it must be ungrateful to ask anything more of you."

"Piffle," she returned, patting Sarah's cheek affectionately. "It seems all I have given you is an unsuitable wardrobe." Sighing, she explained herself. "I thought it would help you find a husband."

"I own I am wishful of avoiding the necessity of donning a spinster's cap," Sarah said, laughing a little. "But I am not so desperate as to accept Mr. Repton's offer."

The Countess emitted a regretful sigh. "You seem to be determined to avoid setting your cap for any gentleman.'

Sarah raised her chin defiantly.

"Do not set your jaw, obstinate girl," scolded the Countess. "What other reason can you have for turning down every eligible offer you have received since your come-out?"

The Marchioness raised her eyebrows questioningly. But Sarah was stunned by her godmother's vulgar and uncharacteristic enquiry. Her mouth dropping open, she attempted to cover it with a hand, as though she had committed the social solecism of yawning in the presence of the Regent. When she had regained her power of speech, she said, "If I have displeased you, Godmama, I ask your forgiveness." She raised her hands imploringly. "I cannot believe you would want me to accept proposals from old men, or gamesters, or rakeshames, merely to gain the ambition of every female."

"Which of these unflattering qualities do you ascribe to my son?" enquired the Countess, as she came imperiously to her feet.

"I beg your pardon, ma'am?"

Lady Pemberton advanced upon her until they stood toe to toe. "Is my son in his dotage, does he gamble, or do you consider him a libertine?"

"No, he is none of those things," Sarah replied, retreating nervously behind a pink marble-topped table. "But I did not take his offer seriously; and now, I think he would not take me."

Lady Pemberton heaved a tremendous sigh and, pressing her palms together as though she were suppressing a violent impulse, said, "For such a brilliant girl, you can be impossibly dull. The man is in l . . . "

"Now, Elizabeth," cautioned the Marchioness, tapping her walking stick on the carpet for attention. "Young people, even brilliant ones, must discover some things for themselves. I did not come here to carry tales, or meddle in something which does not concern me, but to discuss an endowment. Do you wish to make your goddaughter's dream come true, or must you keep raising objections which only obstruct her happiness?"

Lady Pemberton's mouth opened and closed several times as if she were weighing the consequences of defying the Marchioness. At last she folded her lips together, returned to her chair and placed her hands in her lap, saying, "Very well, Letitia. We shall listen to your proposal."

Sarah came out of hiding and placed herself in a chair beside Lady Blake. The Marchioness appearing by her now-gracious smile to be satisfied that she had gained not only everyone's attention, but also their cooperation, pronounced the earthshaking decree, "We shall make a gift of ten thousand."

"What? You will break me!" shrieked Lady Pemberton, who began to fan herself at a furious tempo.

"That is more than I should need for ten schools," Sarah protested.

"My dear, you must do a thing right or not do it a'tall," Lady Blake chided. "Elizabeth, these pinch-penny ways are not like you. I daresay your goddaughter's wardrobe cost half that."

"Well, nearly," Lady Pemberton allowed. Then, submitting to her friend's quelling look, she said, "All right. I'll not complain again. Only I should rather spend the money upon her wedding."

Sarah laughed, but knew, from Lady Pemberton's furrowed brow, that her godmother still had her doubts. What had she been about to tell her before Lady Blake cut her off? Certainly not that the Earl was in love with her. If he were, why hadn't he told her? She had all she could do to attend to her benefactresses as they argued the organizational points of the school. When they set her to work composing an offer of employment to Mrs. Chitham, she threw away three sheets of paper before she could write anything except her beloved's name. Only a stern reminder to herself that he might very well not return her affection brought her romantic wishes to heel and allowed her to write a hopeful letter to the lady upon whose capable shoulders she was entrusting the operation of her school.

The letter dispatched, she applied herself to the now odious task of waiting until a reply could be obtained. What if Mrs. Chitham were already happily employed? What if she had changed her mind completely and gone home to Cheshire?

In time, however, her fears proved to be groundless. Mrs. Chitham returned a grateful note by the same footman who had delivered Sarah's letter. She would be happy to accept the position, had been hoping for this very offer, said everything that must please Sarah and satisfy their bene-factresses as to the suitability of Sarah's choice in headmis-tress for Fair Meadow School. An invitation to join them for the evening's entertainment at Vauxhall was dispatched to Mrs. Chitham immediately. Sarah was satisfied that the large party which was now being assembled for the plea-sure garden must require her constant presence and pre-clude that meeting with her knave.

=== 15 ===

BEFORE LADY BLAKE left Pemberton House, Sarah received a note from Edward. He had broken his plans for the evening and wished to know whether he might accompany the party to Vauxhall. Blushingly, she scribbled a note in return, saying she could not be happier than to have his escort.

Tonight was the first evening she would appear on Edward's arm. She wanted to dazzle him.

Requesting her godmother and the Lioness to excuse her, she retired upstairs to devote the rest of the afternoon to her toilette, an indulgence of which Trent was taking full advantage.

The steaming, fragrant bath, pedicure, and manicure left her feeling euphoric, as if she were aglow. While Trent was blissfully arranging her mistress's thick blonde locks and prescribing the most delicate treatments and artifices to enhance her delicate colouration and natural comeliness, Sarah could not stem her rising excitement. She hoped Edward would be pleased with her.

"My goodness," she said, when her maid finally allowed her to view the effect of her afternoon's work. "Trent, you are an artist."

Trent beamed. "Thank you, Miss. It was a pleasure, I assure you."

Stunned by her transformation from a rather ordinary-looking—in her own estimation—young woman to a dazzling beauty, Sarah pirouetted before the pierglass, disbelieving the image which was reflected. She was strikingly dressed in a gown of shimmering white crepe lisse that draped etherally over an underdress of sapphire blue shot silk. Her blonde hair, disposed in light loose ringlets, softly framed her face. Behind, her long locks were plaited off her neck, and caught in a net of lace and sapphires that twinkled like ensnared stars.

"I have not appreciated the depth of your talents," Sarah apologized, returning her gaze onto her abigail. "Why have you not left me for a fashionable lady?"

As Trent finished setting her pots and brushes in their proper places, she answered in a shaking voice. "Miss, are you dissatisfied with my work?"

Realising she had unwittingly hurt Trent's feelings, Sarah quickly replied, "No, Trent. Not dissatisfied." She stole another glance at her image before she turned back on the mirror. "I am rather awed by it. I never knew I had this in me."

Exhaling a satisfied sigh, Trent said, "I did, Miss. That's why I stayed."

Sarah folded her abigail in a quick, grateful embrace, then glided to the door, promising, "From now on, your talents will not go unnoticed or unappreciated."

Blushing, Trent said, "Thank you, Miss. But I hope you will not go unnoticed. It is high time you broke a heart or two."

Sarah halted on the landing, turning a mischievous smile towards her abigail. "I do not wish to break a heart. I only hope Edward will recognise me."

A well-loved voice spoke behind her. "Do my eyes deceive me? Is this the Sparkler?" When she turned, holding out her hands in delight, he clasped them both and kissed her cheek. "No, thank heaven, it is only Sarah. I can be myself tonight."

"I thought the Sparkler had enchanted you," she teased.

"She did," he replied, folding her hand through the crook of his elbow. "But I have come to prefer the affection of a lady who has a warmer heart."

"I hope I may soon wish you happy," Sarah said, her smile undiminished by his confession.

He guided her downstairs, where they joined Lady Pemberton and their guests, The Viscountess Severn, her daughters and their escorts, Lady Blake, and Mrs. Chitham. "I hope no one will object if I join the party." Everyone was quick to assure the Earl that he was a welcome addition to the party, but no one expressed their gratification in a manner more pleasing to the Earl than Sarah's rapturous smile.

"Sarah!" Phoebe declared, hugging her cousin. "Your god-mother says we must expect good news tonight!" She turned to the Baron, smiling at the gentle brown-haired gentleman, and said, "Imagine, Philip; more announcements."

"Phoebe," Lady Severn said quellingly, her rouged cheeks becoming so infused with colour that she gave the appearance of one susceptible to apopletic fits. "Not yet, my dear," she said with an effort. "We are only come together."

"Yes, Mama," Phoebe said without glancing at her parent. Sarah noticed her cousin's gaze was too full of her Baron to care about her mother's vexation.

"It is too much to hope that your cousin's news will overshadow yours, of course," Lady Severn continued. "In fact, I cannot see why she has not told me when I can expect her to come live with me."

"How good of you to want me still," Sarah said, an ironical smile lifting the corner of her mouth. "But I am certain you would regret having me as a constant companion."

Lady Severn tried to pooh-pooh her niece's observation, but was overruled by both of her daughters. "You know she is right, Mama," said Chloe, with her usual want of tact. "You would be laid low with a constant megrim." Phoebe jabbed an elbow in her sister's ribcage. "Ow!" Chloe complained, rubbing her abused side. "What did I say?"

Major Brown whispered a discreet warning into her little pink ear. Chastened, Chloe murmured, "Beg pardon, Sarah. If my mama suffers the headache, I am certain it will not be your doing. She has them all the time."

Sarah was about to assure her plump and red-faced cousin that she had not taken offence to her thoughtless comment, when Mabb made his solemn announcement that dinner awaited them. Major Brown rubbed his hands together and said in a heartfelt voice, "Thank God we eat. A man c'ld starve at Vauxhall."

Chloe tapped his fingers with her fan and playfully chided him. "That's not what you told me; what of music and lover's kisses?" She blushed behind her fan, seemingly aware that the confession she had made was not the sort one disclosed before one's mother.

Lady Severn did not let her daughter's lapse pass unreproached. "Chloe," she said, in an uncharacteristic moment of restraint, "I cannot like such talk; it sounds so fast. Not at all the thing."

"But no harm has been done, Anne," said Lady Pemberton, ushering her friend into the dining room after the Marchioness. "And Major Brown is right. When you are young, it does seem that one may thrive on kisses. Indeed," she continued, "Who can willingly give up such sustenance?"

"Stop talking fustian, Elizabeth. You will encourage my girls in unseemly behaviour," Lady Severn replied sotto voce. Then, for the edification of the young people, she continued more loudly, "I was never happier than when the Viscount took his odious attentions elsewhere. Our relations were much more convenient then." That the rest of the company had fallen silent during her confession, she seemed unaware. But when none made any further move towards the groaning board, she glanced towards the open door and snapped, "Well, I, for one am hungry. Are you going to eat or not?"

The guests rushed forwards, filling their plates with sustaining refreshment and the air with impetuous chatter, leaving Edward and Sarah in possession of the drawing room. They regarded one another. Of one accord they sprang from the settee as if it had become a bed of nails.

"Will you have something?" he offered, indicating the open doorway and the assembled diners.

"Nothing, thank you," Sarah replied, placing herself abruptly upon the cushion she had just vacated. She was hungry for only one thing, but good breeding prohibited her from requesting him to indulge her appetite for a kiss. When he retook his seat, she nervously urged, "Pray, do not, on my account, forego the dinner my godmother has set out."

He smoothed the front of his white brocade waistcoat and said, "For what I crave, bread and water offer no satisfaction."

She looked so surprised that he enfolded her fingers in a reassuring handclasp, prompting her enquiry, "The Sparkler?" He confessed, "I told you her mystery no longer holds me enchanted."

Sarah was about to tell him everything, when her aunt returned to the drawing room. "You will be left behind," she said in a quelling voice.

On Lady Severn's heels came Lady Pemberton. "Anne, I wish you will let well enough alone."

"So do I," said Edward, raising Sarah to her feet. "But since we do not wish to be left behind, we must finish our talk later." His readiness to depart seemed to satisfy Sarah's aunt, for she hurried to take her place among the rest of the party.

Upon entering the pleasure garden from the gateway through the manager's house, Sarah paused on Edward's arm as she looked down the Grand Walk and its stately avenue of elms. Behind them, quivered Lady Severn, sputtering fury because her carriage had not been discharged of its occupants first. "Does she think we do not wish to get a glimpse of the Colonade?" she hissed in a vicious aside to her older daughter.

"But I can see it perfectly well," Phoebe declared, clinging delightedly to her baron's arm. "Oh, do you hear the musicians?"

"Who cannot hear them must be deaf," carped her mother, covering her ears as protection from the din of Handel's Water Music. "I suppose we must join the promenade."

"It will allow us the opportunity of seeing the sculptures and ruins," said Lord Cawford as he offered his left arm to Lady Severn. She declined to crowd the couple, but called for Elizabeth to walk with her.

"I suppose I must," sighed that lady. "Will you accompany us, Lady Blake, Mrs. Chitham?" The two ladies pronounced themselves willing, and linked arms. "Do take good care of my goddaughter, Edward. I'll not be wanting her to wander down the Dark Walk alone."

Sarah began to shush her godmother, but Edward laughed as he sent his mother on her way. "Rest assured I will not lose her, Mother. We have unfinished business to talk over."

"And you're telling us we shall be in the way," laughed Lady Pemberton.

"In the most polite way I can devise," he replied, before adding in a voice meant only for his mother's ears, "Pray, keep Sarah's meddlesome relative occupied. She has cultivated the unnerving habit of popping up at the most inauspicious moment."

Assuring him she had perfectly taken his meaning, Lady Pemberton swept the Viscountess down the Grand Walk with Lady Blake and Mrs. Chitham in tow.

Sarah watched the ladies walk arm in arm towards the supper boxes, then turned a smiling gaze onto the Earl. "Very neatly done," she congratulated him. "I can think of no one upon whose arm I would rather lean than yours." She was pleased with the manner in which her compliment swelled his chest. But she could not help teasing. "What a pity you are not in the company of your Sparkler."

"If you think I shall spend the evening ogling other ladies to find her, you are mistaken," Edward replied. "The lady at my elbow sparkles quite enough to please me."

Sarah could find nothing in his address with which to

find fault. He was everything that was pleasing in a companion, even if he was indulging in a bit of flummery. That was, she realised, part of the charm of Vauxhall; it was all of a piece with the fabulous statuary, colossal ruins, and fragrant bowers past which they were walking.

Thousands of lights twinkled like stars come to roost amid the foliage that edged the broad walks. Thinking the garden was like a faery land, Sarah persuaded herself that dreams of happy endings might actually come true tonight. Her school was well on its way to becoming reality. She was content to walk forever on the Earl's arm, but in due time he guided her towards the Grove where the orchestra and Mrs. Bland, the popularly affecting soprano, were beginning the evening's concert of sixteen pieces.

Mrs. Bland convincingly trilled the songs which illuminated the torments of unhappy sweethearts—unrequited love, lover's quarrels, lost love, love's death. The performance was not to Sarah's taste, but she was not so hard of heart that she was left dry-eyed at the conclusion of a particularly affecting number. Like numerous other young ladies, she dabbed at streaming eyes, and hoped as she glanced nervously around the sobbing company, that the tears she had shed had not left her cosmetics smeared.

Singularly affected himself by what he nevertheless considered the manipulative delivery of an overly sentimental ballad, Edward pressed his folded handkerchief to his nose and eyes and judged himself far gone in love to have been overcome by the singer's quavering over vanquished lovers. He was tired of the game he and Sarah had been playing. Moreover, after having endured the various tales of woe with which Mrs. Bland had wrung her audiences' hearts, Edward was determined that he and Sarah should at last be happily in love.

He kept her hand tucked within the crook of his arm all evening, except when they were dancing or partaking of the late supper of muslin-thin slices of ham and dwarfed chickens. Sarah had no opportunity of slipping away from the party, even had she wished to keep her published assignation. The hour was growing late; soon cannonfire would herald the commencement of the celebrated Naumachia.

Already couples were strolling towards the reservoir where miniature ships of the line were moored in preparation for the sea battle. Chloe and her Major, and Phoebe and her Baron had separated themselves from the party and were making their way down the crowded avenue. Offering his hand, Edward suggested he and Sarah find a comfortable spot to watch the impending battle.

Sarah placed her hand in his, and came to her feet willingly. "Only," she said as he guided her down the Grand Walk, "I own I have no wish to see this miniature battle."

He halted their steps and turning to face her, clasped both her hands. "No?"

She shook her head. "Will you walk with me?"

"Of course," he said, guiding her through the Grove towards the Grand Cross Walk which intersected every avenue in the garden. They wandered past silent sentinels of stone and pictorial tributes to love's labour lost, all illuminated with the celestially inspired light of Mr. Tyer's ingenious lanterns. But they might have been strolling down a country lane for all the attention they paid the artistic display.

In the shadow of the Temple of Venus, they halted and faced one another as each said at the same time, "I have not been completely honest with you." For a moment they stared at one another, then Sarah dropped her gaze to one of her slippers with which she was scuffing the edge of the path. Edward was staring at his own feet, then, rubbing a hand through his thick black hair, said, "I am feeling remarkably tongue-tied."

"That's not like you," she said, still without looking at him.

Suddenly a rocket burst overhead, lighting the air with a brilliant burst of colour. Sarah clung to him, felt his grip tighten, but then he crumpled at her feet. "Edward?" she cried, "Edward!" Kneeling in the gravel beside him, she felt instinctively for injuries. He was groaning already and holding his head as though he had been struck. "Oh, my darling," she said, cradling his head. "You've been hurt."

In the fading light of the dying illumination, a black-caped individual stepped from the darker shadows. "Looks like your gentleman has been hurt," he said helpfully. Kneeling beside her, he went through the motions of checking for obvious injuries, then stood. "You'd best go for help," he suggested.

"I cannot leave him," she protested.

"I know you think you must remain at your gentleman's side," said the interloper in an urgent tone. "But really it would be better for me to stay here, while you sought the rest of your party."

"Are you certain?" She pressed a trembling hand to her lips.

"Trust me," he said, holding out his hand to lift her to her feet. "Your gentleman will be safe while you are gone."

"But I do not know the way back," she confessed, feeling quite foolish that she had not paid more attention to the path she and Edward had taken.

"Quite simple, really. That direction." The muffled stranger indicated a path to Sarah's right. "Can't take you more than five minutes. I'll take care of the gentleman."

She turned back to Edward. He was clutching her arm with weakened fingers. "I shall get help, darling," she whispered, kissing his pale lips. "You must rest here. I promise I shall return immediately with the Baron and the Major."

"Hurry," urged the interloper. He placed an arm around Edward's shoulders. "I've got him. Run for help, Miss," he said. As his weight was shifted from Sarah's arms into the stranger's, Edward groaned. "Hurry!"

Sarah leapt to her feet, taking several steps down the path. "You're certain this is the way?"

"Yes, go!" The stranger's exigent tone spurred her to

action. Picking up her skirt, she dashed down the path, oblivious to the stones which were cutting through the delicate soles of her elegant slippers. As she rounded a corner, she collided with another dark clad man. "Thank heaven!" she breathed. "Will you come with me?" she implored, tugging upon his arm. "—Lord Pemberton has been hurt! I did not wish to leave him, only I had to."

"Lead on," he replied, indicating the path ahead. Frantic that Edward must think she had abandoned him, Sarah ran down the walk without first allowing herself to become oriented to her surroundings. She did not realise she was going in the wrong direction until she came to a bordering hedge which was not lighted by the ethereal lanterns.

"We are lost," she said, glancing towards the treetops. "I came from the Temple of Venus." Through the twinkling lights, she saw a rooftop which seemed familiar. "See? Over there."

"Yes. But we are not returning in that direction."

"Who are you?" she demanded, when he advanced.

"Have you forgotten? We had an appointment."

"You must be mistaken," she replied, her heart pounding fearfully.

"No," he said. "I was under the impression we were to discuss a marriage proposal."

Sarah pulled out of his grasp, stumbling a few steps down the path. "Charles?"

He followed in her wake, asking, "What are you afraid of, Sarah?"

"Nothing," she said, retreating a few more steps into the darkness. "I wish you will help Edward. He has hit his head."

"I hit him." Mr. Repton kept advancing upon her, driving her towards a narrow, overgrown lane where the lights ended.

"But why?" she asked, stumbling over a root. His arm snaked around her waist, keeping her from falling.

"He was in the way," Mr. Repton replied. When she

stifled a frightened cry, he waved his free hand and said, "Never worry; I did not kill him. I have no wish to fly the country."

"I wish you will leave," she countered.

"Why should I?" he enquired. "Tomorrow I intend to be a landowner." He drew out a folded paper. "Special license."

"That signifies nothing," she said, knowing she must keep him talking until Edward came to his senses. She could defy him, but realised she would only make him more determined if she said, "I will not." Instead, she said, "You will only hold Fair Meadow in trust."

"Ah, yes; for our children," he replied in a maddeningly unruffled tone of voice. "I fear that is a forlorn hope, my dear, as I have no intention that we should bring encumbrances into the world. Marriage in name only, you know." He was carrying her down the narrow path. The sound of cannonfire and aerial bombs was fading into the distance, until the rumble sounded more like distant, threatening thunder than the roar of battle. Finally, he halted their progress, setting her feet upon the damp grass, and said, "You have been spending the evening with my aunt."

"Lady Blake," she said.

"Yes. A pillar of Society," he intoned sarcastically. "And a good friend as long as you fit her bill of respectability."

"How can you say that? She sent you to Eton," Sarah protested, searching in the darkness for the Earl.

"Yes, and bought my commission, and set me up in the world when I sold out." He laughed bitterly. "Are you going to tell me I'm an ungrateful wretch?"

"No," she said. "You know better than I who you are. Only, you cannot believe I shall marry you now, after you have hurt Edward and abducted me."

"I have every reason to believe it," he replied, dragging her once more towards the farthest reaches of the garden. "When we return to Pemberton House in the morning, you will have no choice. Your friends will no longer receive you."

His threats were frightening her. Where was Edward? Desperately she peered into the darkness for a glimpse of his beloved face. She saw nothing but shadows, branches nodding in the warm summer breeze, as though corroborating his dire warnings.

"You know I am right, Sarah, and yet you still deny me. Why? I am the only friend left you. Why will you not come willingly with me?"

She turned a disbelieving gaze upon him. He made it sound as though she had done him the injury. "I will not come with you," she declared, "Because I do not love you, Mr. Repton."

"It is because I am not a gentleman," he said bitterly.

"As you say," Sarah replied. "A gentleman is not necessarily born; some are made, or at least make themselves."

"We'll see," he said, hauling her down the path once more. This time, she did not scruple to follow meekly, but began to kick at him.

Despite her struggles, they soon came to the end of the path. Beyond the curtain of greenery, Sarah heard the scrape of a key in a lock, and realised he had found an unused entrance, and that he had an accomplice. He was going to spirit her away! Edward might never find her. As they moved towards the gate, Sarah hid her face to keep from being scratched by concealing branches, and did not see the left hook that laid Mr. Repton low. But she heard the blow and saw him fall to the ground like cut timber. Immediately, she was pulled into a strong, protective embrace. "Sarah, my dear," Edward called. "I'm here. You're safe now."

She flung her arms about his neck, never intending to let him go. "Edward! I knew you'd come," she said, "I knew it!"

He was pressing kisses on her damp eyelids, and her lips. Between kisses, he replied, "Then your confidence must have done for both of us." Then he held her away from him as if to assure himself that she was safe in his arms. "I thought I should never see you again."

At their feet, Repton groaned.

"Is he alive?" she asked. The Earl leaned over him.

"Yes. But he'll have a headache when he awakens. Come with me," he urged, leading her through the open gate and placing her within a closed carriage.

"Where are we going?" she enquired.

"Home," he replied, giving the direction to the hired coachman. Then he climbed into the coach beside her.

"Will he take us where we wish to go?" she asked as the vehicle jerked into motion.

"I should hope so," Edward replied, tucking her comfortably under his shoulder. Folding an arm around her he said, "I paid him enough to earn his loyalty."

His remark served to remind her that she had a confession to make. She began to pick at her ruined scarf. "I have not been completely honest with you."

"I believe this is where I lost you," he jested. He hugged her to his side, as though worried that he might again lose her. "Sarah, you need confess nothing to me."

"Yes, I must," she insisted. "We cannot always be pretending to be someone we're not."

"Have you been pretending with me?" he enquired sternly.

Without raising her head, she nodded. Then, turning pale eyes upon him, she said, haltingly, "I am the Sparkler." His shoulders began to shake. She wondered how badly she had hurt him with her deception. Turning to him, she pleaded, "My Lord, can you forgive me?"

In the intermittent light from the oil lanterns outside, Sarah saw him smile. "I think it is rather for you to forgive me," he assured her as he withdrew from his pocket a playing card. "You see, I have known of your masquerade since the evening of the masked ball—I suspected before I found this."

"Did you?" she cried. "Then you took my card! Why . . . "

"I decided to let you dangle awhile."

"I thought Charles had it. That is why I had to consider his proposal. You see, he knew about my masquerade."

"No, did he?" Edward's arm tightened around Sarah's shoulder. "Do you think I would have let you run off with that blackguard?"

"I didn't know." She gazed fretfully into his face. "He told me my school was a forlorn hope unless I married him." She buried her face in Edward's exquisitely tailored coat.

"Little fool," he said, giving her a loving shake. "How could you, after your brave speech to me? What happened to your resolution never to marry, but for love?"

"You are infuriating," she declared, turning her face from him. "You did not threaten me, or torment me with . . . "

"No, I merely offered to be your friend, which tormented me," he returned. "As a matter of fact, I believe we are better suited to be married than friends."

Involuntarily, her heartbeat quickened in response to his suggestion. "Do you?" she asked, gazing cautiously at him.

"Do you not think so? Friends invariably agree on everything; spouses rarely do." He fell silent for a long time.

"Well, we do not disagree, exactly. Only," she shrugged her drooping shoulders, "we do not always get on."

"No," he agreed. "Nevertheless, I wish you will marry me."

"Will you not dislike having such a disagreeable wife?"

"How can you think that?" he demanded. "I have discovered a way to make you happy."

"Have you?" she enquired, smiling irresistibly when he crushed her to his chest and kissed her. When he released her, she marvelled breathlessly, "Yes, I believe you have."

"Who do you think decided to found your school and enlisted Mrs. Chitham?"

"You? You found Mrs. Chitham?" She regarded him with renewed admiration. "But why did you not tell me?"

"Sarah, you are a willful woman, and I love you." He placed a kiss upon her upturned nose. "Can you honestly tell me you would not have thrown my assistance back at me?"

"Well," she said, thoughtfully twisting a button on his waistcoat. "I don't think I would have. I didn't think I could throw Mr. Repton's offer away." She grasped his lapels and shook them vehemently. "Really, Edward, you cannot know how desperate I've been. Everybody telling me I'm too young and unsettled to be a proper guardian, or such a settled spinster that I cannot possibly tell girls how to get along in the Marriage Mart. Even you."

"You will have a lifetime to convince me of my mistake," he teased gently. "And I shall have a lifetime to convince you I shall not go a-wandering about looking for my mythological Sparkler."

"Are you truly content with me?" she asked incredulously.

"I am satisfied beyond all expectations," he said. "I am madly in love with a sensible woman who is not above hoaxing the world. And I am beginning to understand that marriage with you will certainly not be convenient."

"Do you think so?" She was momentarily nonplussed: "Do you wish to marry me, or not?"

He chuckled affectionately. "Absolutely. I love you, Sarah."

She took his face in both her hands. "Dear Edward, after all I have done, how can you love me?"

He shrugged as though explanation were beyond his capabilities. "I am eminently reasonable, but I cannot explain it. But marry you I will, if you'll have me."

"How soon can we be married?" she enquired.

"After tonight's narrow escape, I have no intention of having a breath of scandal taint our marriage or mar the opening of your school. We shall publish our intentions in the Gazette, have the banns read in church and accept the felicitations and good wishes of everyone who chances to receive a notice of our impending nuptials."

"But that will take forever. My school . . . "

He placed his forefinger upon her lips. "Never fear, my love. My mother and Lady Blake are entirely serious about the endowment. They and Mrs. Chitham will see that Fair Meadow is outfitted while we are on our honeymoon."

"You are too good," she said, overcome at last by the depth of his love.

"That is far different cry than first I heard cross your lips," he teased, placing his hands tenderly on either side of her face. "You must be blind to my faults."

"Not blind, Edward. I see you in a different light," she replied generously, and received a kiss as a reward. The coach drew to a halt outside Pemberton House. "I love you with all my heart."

"Then we must not tarry here any longer," he said, throwing open the door and handing her to the sidewalk.

After he had let them inside and ushered them into the privacy of his library, Sarah, leaning her head upon his shoulder, said in a serious tone, "You are too good to me, Edward. I have no right to ask anything more of you."

"You may have whatever is in my power to bestow," he said, lightly. "Riches, jewels, children, what will you have?"

"Honesty, my love. We may hoax the world, but we must never again hoax one another."

"Very well, dearest," he said, settling her beside him on the leather settee. "We shall thrive on honesty."

"We shall grow in love," she replied, turning up her lips in invitation. As he obliged her with another kiss, she knew she had been waiting all of her life for this one moment, and every moment which must follow.

If you would like to receive details of other Walker Regency Romances, please write to:

Regency Editor
Walker and Company
720 Fifth Avenue
New York, NY 10019